FULL MOON

JENNY SULLIVAN

Full Moon

Pont

For:
Daisy, Tove, Catrin, Dylan, Kieran, Izzie, Cass
and also Ellie Mills
with love.

Published in 2011 by Pont Books, an imprint of
Gomer Press, Llandysul, Ceredigion, SA44 4JL

ISBN 978 1 84851 396 9

A CIP record for this title is available from the British Library.

This book is published with the financial support of the
Welsh Books Council.

Printed and bound in Wales at
Gomer Press, Llandysul, Ceredigion

CHAPTER ONE

'**S**EE YOU tomorrow, dear, all right? It's a bit difficult just now.' Aunty Gwen tried to shut the door in my face.

'Aunty? Are you trying to get rid of me?' I tried to sneak a look inside the house but, for a wrinkly, she was, like, really strong. And today, totally weird.

Don't get me wrong: I love my family to bits, but no one could call them *normal*. Until now, though, I'd thought Aunty Gwen had enough sarnies for a picnic – at least a quick one. She's more a crumbly than a wrinkly, but she's always sort of made sense. Now, I was beginning to wonder.

Mind, walking a mile with a heavy bag and then not being let into the house for some light refreshments is not on, in my book. If I'm frank, however (and I'm not Frank – I'm actually Nia – pleased to meet you) I'm one of those people for whom EVERYTHING goes wrong if it possibly can.

Take 'work experience', as decreed by school. Nothing to it, right? You spend a couple of weeks getting up at some ungodly hour to go to some rotten office, factory or school on the other side of the town. Then you, like, totally waste your time following people around and doing rubbish jobs like photocopying and stuffing paper in envelopes.

Then, when you've put up with that for two whole weeks, *they* write a report to your teachers that says: 'Oh, she was really great at doing rubbish jobs'. Then you forget about work experience and try to decide what you're *really* going to do with your life, when you've finally finished school.

My work experience, a deadly two weeks in a solicitor's office, was fairly dire even by my standards. For a start I blew up the photocopier, got blamed for crashing their computer system *just by sitting next to a person using a laptop*, and then managed to tip coffee into the senior partner's lap in the middle of an important meeting. OK, the coffee was a bit on the hot side – but there was no need for language like that, was there? Anyway, I wasn't paid to serve coffee. Come to think of it, I wasn't paid!

The report they sent to my school was fairly diplomatic – especially where they filled in the bit that asked about 'long-term suitability for the employment experience undertaken'. They wrote: 'The employer who could get Nia to work for them would be extremely fortunate' ... Which can be taken two ways if you think about it. But my head of year, Mrs Pritchard, knows me. She gave me a long look, and said, 'Perhaps the only safe place to send you for work experience, Nia dear, might be a well-padded cell.' I told her I hadn't messed up on purpose, but I don't think she believed me.

She knows, you see, that my whole family is as mad as a box of frogs. Mrs P is due (overdue, probably, unless teaching our family has prematurely aged her) for retirement. Over the years she's suffered both my parents and my sister, and she will get to teach my crazy little brother too if she can't escape to an old folks' home in time.

My family consists of Dad, Mam, big sister Ceri, little brother Satan (sorry, Steffan) which of course makes me the Middle Child, so naturally I've got problems. It's a well-known fact that middle children carry a heavy burden. We have a different – no, unique – outlook on life.

My mam is possibly the most totally <u>un</u>-motherly mother on the planet. I love her to bits – she's my mam – but she is such a total loser in the mam stakes she should have a big red 'L' tattooed on her forehead! I mean, she's what she calls thirty-mumble-mumble (i.e. forty-five) – but she still has this dream of Making it Big on the telly. She once had a tiny non-speaking part in some old soap, just after she left college. She'd done a drama course as part of her English degree, and got bitten by the acting bug. She's never had another part or an audition, ever – or even an agent willing to take her on. Because *she can't act!* If you think 'wooden' and 'fake' and 'hopelessly unconvincing' and then double it, you might get some idea of how bad she is – but acting is what she *wants and wants and wants* to do. She refers to her two-minute appearance (I think she was carried into *Casualty* on a stretcher, having been squashed by a milk float or something) as 'my career in television'. She's convinced that one day some telly producer is going to see a re-run of 'her' episode on some extra-terrestrial channel and scream: 'That's the woman I want to star in my new hit soap series!' I mean, it's *so* not going to happen!

My dad is really sweet and more or less normal, if a bit over-Mam'd. He's survived mainly by switching off and has made not-listening an art form. That and hiding in his shed.

My big sister Ceri (my only sister – one's plenty, *diolch*!) was hiding behind the door, down in the basement, in a pit, behind a bulletproof screen AND wearing a biohazard suit when they handed out common sense. She's so clever, she's got A-stars, like, coming out of her *ears*, but her common-sense qualifications are sort of X-minus.

Then there's Steffan, who is nine. Outwardly, a perfectly normal small boy, i.e., irritating, annoying, infuriating, smelly, disgusting. You can tell where he is by the mess. Except . . . Except he's usually someone or something else. Sometimes he's a Superhero, sometimes a Robot, sometimes an Animal. He Goes-Through-a-Phase until he gets bored with it. The Spiderman phase was really, really trying, especially if you aren't over-keen on spiders, like me, and you don't want to *know* about his Pig phase. I love him, really, though – especially when he's away from home on school trips.

So, that's the immediate family. The extended family isn't much better – I have three aunts and two uncles, and every single one of them is a card-carrying, fully paid-up, Olympic level nut-job. But for the moment, I'll just stick with Aunty Gwen. One dire experience at a time, that's enough to be going on with.

Which brings me back to where I started. Aunty Gwen. She's a real sweetheart, and always has a supply of chocolates for those who are unfortunately addicted (see my spots?). Aunty Gwen, who, right now, is Not Letting Me In.

Picture me, standing on her doormat, which says *Croeso* in big red letters on a white-and-green background, all very patriotic. Only she's not being welcoming at all. In fact, she's trying to shut the door on my nose, and she's saying, more or less, go away, Nia. So I've got my foot in the door because I'm, like, nosy, and because my mam has sent me round with a bag of goodies like Little Red Riding Hood (and on the subject of LRRH, who sends a kid out wearing come-and-eat-me red into a wolf-infested forest?). Aunty Gwen threaded an arm through the crack in the door and tried to grab the carrier bag from my hand. I hung on.

'See you tomorrow, Nia, is it?' she panted, trying to force the door shut.

'Why not let me bring it in, Aunty Gwen? It's too heavy for you,' I suggested, quite reasonably, I thought.

'I'm busy. You can't come in!' she said, and managed to grab the carrier bag and push the door shut simultaneously – I just managed to extract my bits in time.

'*Well, good heavens!*' I thought (well, something like that!). I've never, ever known Aunty Gwen to be that unsociable. She's got a mind like a rat-trap, even though she pretends to be a bit on the vague side.

So. What next? I'm not one to take offence, but stuff like this makes me curious, and when I'm curious I'm persistent. I twiddled my hair and bit my thumbnail and thought. Right. She won't let me in through the front, so . . . I shot out the front gate and round the corner to the lane, pushed open the back door in the wall and went in. It is one of those long, narrow Victorian gardens that have a row of bushes halfway up to hide the veggie patch. Too late for blackcurrants or I would have pinched a couple on the way past, purely to save them from the slugs. I peered round the bushes. There were two ways in at the back of the house, either up a short flight of steps to the back porch and kitchen, or down another three to the basement door, which was, I knew from past experience, covered in spiders' webs (see Spiderman/Steffan

9

phobia, above) and usually locked. I couldn't see Aunty Gwen in the kitchen, so I made a break for the door and tiptoed up the steps. The porch door opened when I twisted the knob, and I stepped inside.

It was full of the usual stuff you find in porches and back entries: a basket with some limp weeds, a half-used sack of spuds, some muddy wellies, a garden fork and spade, some bits of hairy string and a damp packet of weedkiller. I sneaked a peek through the glass window in the kitchen door to see if she was inside: she wasn't. I turned the handle slowly, and pushed.

Locked. I said a few naughty words in my head. What now? Ah well. I decided to give the basement door a try, and if that didn't open, give up, although I'm not known for giving up. I went down the mossy steps and tried the handle, but that was locked as well. But then I noticed that the manky mess of cobwebs around the frame was broken, and on the step was a large footprint in dried mud. I stared. Too big a print for Aunty Gwen . . . I thought for a bit, but inspiration didn't arrive (nothing unusual there), and if Aunty Gwen wasn't going to let me in, I might as well go home and return some time when she wasn't expecting me. She'd have to let me in sooner or later, and then I'd find out what was going on.

I wandered back towards our house, off in my own world – until a voice called, 'Oi! Nia?'

Ryan O'Brien, who as well as having the only rhyming name in the entire school, is the current object of my affections. The Love Interest, if you like. (If you don't, stop reading now. It might get mushy. With any luck . . .)

'Hiya, Ryan,' I said, kicking a stray coke can towards him. 'What's occurrin'?'

'Not a lot,' he said, gloomily kicking it back. 'Jamie Roberts has damaged his cruciate ligament, and Shane Williams has got an ingrowing toenail, and I don't even want to think about James Hook's sore knee. Might as well quit now, and be done with it.'

The object of my affections, like I say. Unfortunately, all *his* affections are directed towards rugby. Welsh rugby, that is. He's on a high when they're winning, and almost manic with depression when they're not. I dare say he'll discover girls one day – and I'd really, really like to be around when he does.

'Oh, Ryan,' I bleated. 'Don't worry! They're tough. They'll be fit again in no time.' I booted the can back at him. It was contact of sorts, but on a scale of one to ten, it wasn't much more than a minus-three, was it?

'Oh, aye,' – he gloomily punted the can towards me again – 'but will they be fit in time for the Six Nations, that's what I want to know. Cruciate ligaments take time, and sore knees – well there's no telling what that might lead to.'

'No, there isn't,' I replied doggedly, not knowing if cruciate ligaments were in the brain or the belly button but desperately trying to keep the conversation going. 'Look on the bright side, Ry – it's months till the Six Nations, right? Stacks of time to get fit.'

He brightened. 'Aye. True. Carn argue with that.' He glanced up at me, and quickly away again, nonchalantly booting the coke can between the next two lampposts and perilously close to a window.

'Nia, I got tickets for the Scarlets game, Sat'day. Wanna come?'

Do bears poo in the woods? Didn't want to seem too eager, though. I put my head on one side and screwed up my face attractively (well, that's what I was aiming at, anyway!) while I pretended to be thinking about it. Then . . . 'Yeah. Why not? That'd be great, Ryan.'

'F'ntastic! Pick you up Sat'day then? My dad'll drive us down. See you.'

'Yeah, Ryan. See you.'

Then he was off, hooking the can from the gutter and kicking it along the road, hooning it down the Millennium Stadium pitch with the roar of the crowd in his ears, probably. OK, so we were going to a rugby match, and his dad was driving us – but hey, it was a start, right? He could have asked his mate Dubious Mike instead.

That evening I was nice to everyone, Steffan included, even when I found out he'd borrowed my MP3 player without asking. I only thumped him once, and then not very hard. Then when Ceri asked in front of Dad if I had any homework, my only revenge was salt in her bedtime cocoa instead of sugar. Lots of it. She took two big swallows before she noticed.

I was, like, floating all evening, and even sang as I did my maths homework, so it's probably totally wrong. I don't Do maths!

I was just dropping off when I remembered Aunty Gwen and the footprint on the basement step. That was soooooo weeeeeird . . .

CHAPTER TWO

NEXT morning, Monday – school. I couldn't wait to get in and tell my best mate, Mably (whose parents apparently met at a pub called the Cefn Mably and the rest is history) that I had a date with Rhyming Ryan O'Brien.

Her eyes went satisfactorily round. 'You never have!'

'Have too!'

'Where you going? Pictures?'

'Scarlets game, Saturday.'

'Oh.' She screwed up her nose. 'Rugby? That's, like, so unromantic. I mean, a rugby match. But then, Dubious Mike usually goes with him.'

'Exactly. So, is it a date or not?'

'Oh – I s'pose. Mind you, if he's had a bust-up with Mike or something, he'd have a spare ticket. Wouldn't count then, would it?'

Despite official acknowledgement that it was a date, I wasn't expecting Ryan to start holding my hand at break, which was just as well because he didn't. But like I say, it's a start, yeah? He was over by the bike stands with his mates, and from their intent faces they were either talking rugby or maybe discovering how to split the atom with a pencil sharpener. Guess which.

After lunch, double art with Mrs Richards, who's one of the few teachers who don't think I'm a waste of space. Some of them, though I sit in their classes regularly at least twice a week, can't put a name to my face. Mrs Richards, mind, she thinks I have Talent, and is nice to me. I'm working on my first mega-collage. I've done a couple of small ones, but this one is two metres by two metres and I've been working on it for a whole term now, crawling all over the studio floor and getting messy. All summer I collected stuff from the beach, driftwood and shells and bits of blue string (why is there always blue string on beaches?) and I'm attaching this to a brown-and-pale-blue hessian backing, and it's going to look *so* great when it's finished. Mrs Richards says that if it lives up to her expectations, she's going to put it in an exhibition. It's up to me to make sure it does.

I was getting really stuck in – literally – glue and paint all over my hands, face and hair, when the school secretary stuck her head round the door. 'Sorry to disturb you, Mrs Richards,' she stage-whispered. 'Is Nia Roberts in here?'

'Yes?' I said, sticking my head up. Usually when I'm hooked out of classes I'm in trouble, but I couldn't remember doing anything wrong recently. Maybe it was the work-experience solicitors wanting to offer me a Saturday job. Not.

'Phone call, Nia,' she said, holding the door open for me to walk under her arm. She eyed my hands. 'Why don't you have a wash before you touch my nice clean phone?' So I did, despite being desperate to find out who was phoning school, and not my mobile. Dad was away on a course; Mam should be in work, and if there were problems at Steffan's school they'd phone her – so who'd be phoning me?

Marching ahead of me down the echoing corridor to the office, the secretary remarked over her shoulder that personal phone calls in school hours were Not Allowed Except in Emergencies, Nia.

'I know,' I snapped. 'And so does my family, so more than likely it's an emergency, right?' What I was thinking was 'Shut up, you stupid woman and let me worry in peace' but she might have taken offence at that.

I picked up the phone. 'Hello?'

'Hello? Nia?'

'Yes. Who's that?'

'Aunty Gwen, dear.'

'Aunty Gwen? What's the matter? Why are you ringing me at school?'

'I've had a bit of a bump, dear. I'm in hospital. Can you come? I've telephoned Valmai,' – that's my mam – 'but she's not answering.'

'Oh, Aunty? Are you all right? Where are you?' (Daft question.)

'In Casualty, Nia.'

'Don't worry. I'll be there now, soon as I can.'

I put the phone down. 'My aunty's had an accident,' I said. 'She's in the hospital and she wants me with her.'

Mrs Wells sniffed. 'I'd better ask the Head. It's not right, you going. You're just a child. Where are your parents?'

'My parents,' I snapped, 'are both, obviously, unavailable, or she'd have phoned them and not me, wouldn't she?'

'What about your big sister?'

'Oh, come on, Mrs Wells. You know Ceri. Would you send for her in an emergency? Would anyone?' She'd have been running about like a headless chicken.

She saw the sense in that. 'Just a tick, then, Nia. I'll tell

15

the Head.' She whipped through a door and shut it behind her. It opened again shortly after, and the Head emerged. She has a face like a disapproving horse, but she's OK, really.

'Nia? I hope this isn't one of your nefarious schemes.'

'No, Dr Bell, honestly. It's my aunt, really it is.'

'Hmm. Is Mably Jones in school today?' she asked the secretary.

'I believe she is, Dr Bell.'

'In that case . . . Look, Nia, I'll drive you to the hospital. I can't let you go by bus, not if it's an emergency.'

'Oh *thanks*, Dr Bell! Are you sure you can spare the time?'

'Quite sure, dear. Go quickly and get your things. I'll bring my car to the front entrance.'

So the Head went in one direction and I went in another, and we met up outside. I scrambled into her sports car, and we roared out of the school gates. She drove much faster than I'd have expected. Maybe she has Hidden Depths. She stopped at the side entrance to A & E and turned to me. 'Shall I come in with you?'

'No thanks, Dr Bell. I can cope. After all, if Aunty Gwen was OK enough to use the phone, it's not going to be, like, really dire, is it?'

'That's true, I suppose. Well, I do have a governors' meeting this afternoon, so if you're sure –'

'I'm sure. And thanks again. I really appreciate the lift.'

'That's all right, dear. But if you need help, and can't locate your parents, please ring the school.'

'I will,' I promised, leapt out of the car and ran in through the swing doors. There was a busy-looking clerk at reception. So busy that, although I was standing there in front of her, and even though I'm a fairly solid sort of person, she managed not to notice me until I cleared my throat, loudly, and dinged her bell. She glanced up and then back down again. 'Be with you in a minute,' she muttered, and carried on filing. Her nails. At last, she gave me her full attention. Just in time, too. I was about to reach over the counter, grab her tenderly by the nose and rip it off.

'Visiting is the other door, and only between four o'clock and eight. And if you're under sixteen, you can't come in by yourself.'

For goodness' sake! Ceri's nineteen and as dependable as an ice-cream fireguard, but she'd have let her in! 'My aunt is in Casualty,' I said, trying not to grit my teeth.

'Is she?'

'Mrs Furnival. Gwen Furnival.'

The clerk shuffled some papers and looked at some lists. 'Oh yes. So she is. The poor old dear with the GBH, right?'

'GBH?'

'*Grievous* Bodily Harm,' she elaborated smugly.

Grievous, I thought. 'So where is she?'

'I'll ask Sister.' She picked up the phone. There was a short conversation, somewhat grovelling at her end, I'm pleased to say, and she hung up. 'Go through those doors and ask a nurse. Don't you go wandering about: we can't have children wandering around A & E unaccompanied.'

Oh bum to you! I thought, and hurtled through the doors. Luckily there was a nurse there, so I wasn't tempted to go wandering. And I would have, too, just to spite Old Sourpuss on the desk!

'I'm looking for Mrs Furnival, please?'

'Are you the one she phoned?'

'Yes. Is she all right?'

'Well, she's not seriously injured, so don't worry. Come with me, love – she's down here.'

Isn't it amazing how often the people who work at the sharp end of things are so much nicer than the people who don't? I followed the nurse through another set of double doors and down a corridor lined with cubicles, some with the flowery curtains drawn, some open and empty. Smells of antiseptic, murmurs of voices, and a loud male voice: 'Ow!' The nurse stopped at a set of drawn curtains and stuck her head through. 'It's Gwen's niece, Dr Shami.'

'Mrs Furnival can have one visitor,' a voice said. It was a nice, soft, accented voice, and even before I saw its owner, I approved. I hate the way hospitals call old people by their first names. Anyway, the doctor was tiny, and had a smile on her face. My aunt was smiling too, which, right at that moment, was even more important.

'Aunty Gwen, are you all right?'

She was lying on one of those wheelie-trolley things, covered in a white honeycomb blanket, and she looked terrible. She had a black eye, and a cut face, and her normally tidy hair was matted with dirt and blood. Her lip was swollen, and her right arm was in a sling.

'Aunty Gwen, what happened?' To my horror, she began to weep. This wasn't like my aunt at all.

Dr Shami patted her good arm and made shushing noises. The attending nurse handed her a hypodermic syringe and Dr Shami slid it into the butterfly thingy stuck in the back of my aunt's left hand. 'Your poor aunty was attacked,' she said, frowning. 'Some youths attacked her and stole her pension. She is very shocked and we shall have to keep her in hospital for a while. We don't want to take any chances, do we? But you can be very proud of her – what is your name?'

'Nia,' I replied.

'– Nia. She gave an excellent description to the policeman when she was first brought in. But for now she must rest, and very soon I shall send her up to the ward. Would you like to stay with her? There is nothing more I can do for her here, and there are other patients I must see.'

'Of course,' I said. 'Thank you for everything.'

Dr Shami smiled and disappeared through the curtains. Aunty Gwen grabbed me, wincing as the butterfly needle stuck in the back of her hand pulled at the skin. She hung on tightly.

'Nia, I've got to talk to you. It's really important –' she began.

'Shh, Aunty Gwen. I'm sure it can wait. You have to rest now; the doctor said so.'

'It can't wait, Nia. Really it can't. You *must* listen to me.'

Then a porter came in, and I had to stand aside while he tidied up Aunty Gwen's clothes and put them in a plastic bag and gave them to me to hold, and put the cardboard kidney dish on top of the blanket in case she felt sick. 'Just taking your granny up to the ward –' he began.

'My aunty,' I muttered.

'Whatever. You follow me, and you can see her settled in, all right? You comfy, Ma?'

19

Aunty Gwen was drowsy, but not that drowsy. 'I Am Not Your Ma, young man,' she muttered.

'Oh, pardon me for living,' he said, and pushed her in wounded silence from then on. I followed him out of A & E, down a long corridor, up in a lift, down another long corridor, and into a four-bed ward, where a nurse came in and helped him lift Aunty Gwen from the trolley to the bed. When he'd gone, the nurse made Aunty Gwen comfortable, and tucked her up neatly. I wasn't too worried – I assumed it was the effect of whatever happy juice the doctor had pumped into her that was making her sleepy.

'You going to sit with your . . .' – the nurse raised her eyebrows questioningly.

'Aunty,' I explained.

'. . . aunty for a while?'

'If it's all right.'

'Oh, I think so. You look sensible enough, *bach*, even if you are covered in blue paint.'

I'd forgotten that. I'd washed it off my hands, but not my face, and my hair was stiff with it. She slid the curtains back around the bed and left me alone with Aunty Gwen, whose eyelids were drooping.

'Nia?'

'Yes? You were trying to tell me something, Aunty Gwen?'

'Mmmm? Oh, yesssh. There was shome . . . shomething, wasn't there. Oh, – Nia!' Her eyes flew open suddenly. 'Now I remember. You have to –'

But then she was asleep.

20

CHAPTER THREE

WHEN she'd zonked out, I left. The ward sister said the sedative she'd been given would keep her 'under' for hours.

'Come back tonight, love. She'll be back with us by then, I expect. Poor old dear – fancy anyone doing that to her!'

'I know. It makes me want to rip their ears off and stuff them up their . . . '

She gave me an old-fashioned look and smiled. 'I thoroughly agree with you. You don't have to finish *that* sentence!'

I grinned at her, stuck my head back through the curtains for a last look at Aunty Gwen, who was snoring with her mouth open, and headed home. It was half past two, no point in going back to school for double maths, was there? I hopped on a bus outside the hospital. Luckily I'd remembered my door key, because Mam was still out when I got home. I tidied up downstairs, put the breakfast dishes in the dishwasher, and got myself a cheese sandwich and a glass of milk.

Steffan got home first, long before Mam, and since he doesn't have a door key, it was just as well I didn't go back to school, or he'd have been sitting on the doorstep until I got home and let him in. He goes to the primary school up the road, and refuses to be taken or fetched by anyone. The trouble with Mam is that, once she's got rid of him and his

Spidey lunchbox in the morning, she tends to forget he'll be coming home again.

'What you doing home so early?' he demanded. 'You been mitchin'?'

'No, clever clogs, I haven't, and even if I had, it wouldn't be any of your business, so ner.'

'What you doing home, then?'

'Aunty Gwen got mugged! She phoned me from the hospital!'

Steffan's eyes grew round. 'She never! Poor old Aunty Gwen! She all right?'

'Yeah. Some blokes knocked her over and pinched her pension – she's got her arm in a sling and some cuts and bruises and she's shaken up – but she'll be all right.'

'Steenkin' cowards!' he said in his Mexican-bandit accent. 'Eef I could get my 'ands on zem, I'd show zem mugging!'

'Only if you stood on a box,' I pointed out.

'Oh, go on, go on,' he yelled angrily. 'Just because I'm only nine doesn't mean I can't DO stuff, you know! You're always putting me down!'

I know it was rotten, but I couldn't resist it. 'Wouldn't have to put you down very far, Steff, would I? You're only three feet up to start with!' Which was an exaggeration, and unkind, but hey, he's my little brother, right?

Steffan stamped upstairs in a huff and I heard his computer-game thingy start to bleep. He'd come down in a good mood – he always did – he forgot everything after an hour zapping bad guys into neutrons and sub-atomic particles.

Mam came home at half past five, on the same bus as Ceri, and they were arguing as they came through the door, which was nothing new. They both lost interest in their argument once I told them about Aunty Gwen, and Mam started bustling around, tossing fish fingers into a pan and chips in the oven so we could go and see Aunty Gwen in hospital. Dad came in last, at six o'clock, just in time to sit down with us and eat, which is just as well, because otherwise he'd have had to get something from the chippy down the road instead. Poor old Dad: Mam isn't the most efficient mam in the world, but we love her anyway. I think she loves Dad, too, but he knows he usually comes second to her Search-for-Fame-and-Fortune. That evening he was supposed to be taking part in a pub quiz but he didn't moan or complain, just called up the reserve player to go in his place so that he could come with us to see Aunty Gwen. He's a nice bloke, my dad.

We all sat around the telly eating our fish fingers and chips (half a bottle of ketchup on Steff's) and watched the news. We didn't usually – we sat at the table and did it politely and made conversation, even if it was only 'take your elbows off the table' and 'pass the salt, please' – but tonight was special. Sure enough, Aunty Gwen was on the Welsh news! Jamie Owen looked all serious and reported that she'd been mugged outside the post office and was now in hospital, where she was likely to remain for a few days. It made it seem even more unreal, hearing about it on telly, somehow!

Aunty Gwen was sitting up in bed drinking a cup of tea when we arrived for visiting, the crusts of a hospital sandwich on the locker beside her. We'd stopped off at the corner shop and picked up loads of extra supplies to keep her going until they let her out. She looked even worse than she had earlier: her bruises had darkened, and one of her eyes was ringed black: she looked like a lopsided panda. There were long raw scrapes on the elbow and wrist of the arm that was in a sling, her lip had puffed up to twice its size and her hands were shaking so much that she could hardly hold the cup of tea.

'Gwenny!' Mam was off. 'I was utterly devastated when I heard! Are you all right?'

'Oh, for heaven'th thake, Valmai,' Aunty Gwen muttered, her fat lip making her talk funny, 'don't be tho melodramatic. I got mugged. Thtuff happenth.'

I thought that was very trendy of Aunty Gwen – the polite version, too! I grinned at her, and she gave me a most peculiar look in return – her eyebrows sort of wiggling, her eyes looking frantic. 'What?' I asked, and she frowned and shook her head, sort of 'not now!' at me.

'So what happened, Gwenny, love?' Dad, being sensible.

'Yeah, what? Was it a gang of hoodies that surrounded you and beat you up? Did they kick you and stomp you and punch you?' Steffan asked hopefully.

Aunty Gwen gave him a lopsided, puffy grin. 'No, *cariad*. Jutht two of them, but they were big enough to puth me over. Thorted me out good and proper, and thtole my betht handbag, too. *And* my penthion, the wretcheth! But I managed to land a good one on one of 'em with my umbrella before they got away, mind. Made hith ear bleed where I cut it, right by here,' she said with satisfaction, indicating a point halfway down her right ear. 'I really thocked him one!'

'Good for you,' Dad said. 'Did the police –'

'Well, they came and took a thtatement from me when

I wath in Cathualty, but they don't hold out mutth hope of catching them – there'th lotth and lotth of people in the thame boat ath me – oh, damn thith lip of mine! – and half the time they don't ever catth anyone, do they?'

'I bet I could track him down,' Steffan said thoughtfully, 'if you gave me a description, and if I didn't have to go to school tomorrow. I could hang around the post office and look for a scruffy bloke with a cut on his ear who bashes up old ladies –'

'No!' Dad said, at the same time as Aunty Gwen said, 'Who are you calling an old lady?'

Steffan shut up.

So, we gave Aunty Gwen the stuff we'd brought, and some magazines that Mam had picked up in the 'concourse', which is what hospitals call the shopping bit near the entrance, and made small talk until they rang the bell for the end of visiting, and then we said goodbye. The others filed out obediently – but I couldn't go anywhere, because Aunty Gwen grabbed my sleeve and hung on for dear life. The others, not noticing I wasn't tagging along, carried on towards the exit.

I sat down again. 'What's up, Aunty?'

'I want you to do thomething for me, Nia,' she said urgently. 'It'th really important, but you might have to duck out of thchool to do it.'

'No problemo,' I said, and grinned wickedly.

'Nia!' Aunty Gwen said sharply. 'You know that you need proper qualificathionth to get anywhere thethe dayth – look at your thithter wathting her intelligenthe doing a thilly job like that!'

'Yeah, well.' Intelligence? Debatable . . . 'So, what's so important I need to cut school, then, Aunty Gwen?'

'I want you to go to my houthe, and let yourthelf in and – leave thome food on the kitchen table.'

I stared at her. 'Food? Who for? There's only you, and you're in here!'

She frowned. I could almost hear the cogwheels whizzing round. 'Vithitor. I have a vithitor coming. Later. Tomorrow, I mean. Need to leave thome food out.'

'A visitor? How will they get in if you aren't there to open the door? Anyway, you can't let a visitor turn up at an empty house. That'd be awful, and if you leave food out, it'll go off. Who is it? Look, I'll go over tomorrow and hang around until the visitor arrives, and then we'll go over to our house. It's a mess, but it's got to be better than an empty house. Anyway, whoever it is can't get in unless I'm there, right? You can't leave the door unlocked: someone might go in and steal stuff. I'll tell Mam and Dad to expect a visitor –'

'No!' she yelped, and the three other ladies in the ward all turned to stare at her. She lowered her voice. '*No!*' she hissed. '*You muthn't be there. Promithe? And you muthn't tell your mam and dad! Jutht go tomorrow morning, early, and put thome food out. And then go to thchool. All right?*'

I shrugged. 'Whatever you want, Aunty Gwen. But I don't see –'

'Jutht do ath I thay, pleathe, Nia? Go tomorrow morning and leave thome food out.' She lay back on her pillows. 'Will you?'

'OK. Is there food there? Ham or cheese or something? Oh – you'll have to give me a door key so I can get in.'

'There'th a loaf of bread in the fridge, and thome ham. Perhapth you can make thome thandwicheth, and leave them out. That will keep him going for a while.'

Him! my brain registered. That was the point when I suddenly realised that Aunty Gwen was, like, totally concussed. The bash on the head had knocked a screw loose. There wasn't any visitor – I mean, she'd never had visitors before, not as far as I knew. Poor old soul. Maybe I should just humour her.

'Yeth. And there'th a lamb bone in the fridge. You might ath well leave that out, too.'

I patted her hand. 'All right, Aunty. Just leave it to me. Don't worry about a thing.'

'You will do it, won't you, Nia?' Aunty Gwen said. There was a note of something like desperation creeping into her voice.

'Look, don't go upsetting yourself, Aunty,' I soothed her. 'I will, I promise. I'll skip the first session tomorrow – it's only science anyway – and I'll go over and put some food out. Promise. Now, where's your handbag? I'll need the door key.'

'My handbag?'

'Yes – where –?' Then I remembered. 'Oh, no! It got nicked, didn't it, Aunty?'

She sniffled. 'Yeth! I didn't think of that! It wath thtolen by thothe horrible boyth. But you mutht get into the houthe thomehow, Nia – you mutht. It'th really *important.*'

'Don't worry, Aunty Gwen.' I patted her hand. 'I'll break in if I have to – maybe into the basement –'

'No! Not the bathement. *Not the bathement!* Go in through the back door – thmath the window and get the key from the inthide. Mind you don't cut yourthelf though. Clothe the thutters and lock the outer door when you leave. The key ith on the inthide. Take it with you in cathe they don't let me out of here tomorrow.'

And they certainly wouldn't, not if she was still concussed and talking rubbish. 'All right, Aunty Gwen. Now don't you worry about anything at all. Promise?'

'Jutht tho you go round tomorrow. It hath to be tomorrow. Not tonight. If my neighbourth heard you breaking in after dark, you'd have the polithe after you, I exthpect. You don't want that, do you?'

I didn't. But then, I wasn't going anyway, so I said, 'Of course, Aunty!'

Just then a nurse stuck her head round the ward door. 'Visiting's over, I'm afraid. Your aunt needs her rest, dear, so off you go, please. You can come in tomorrow. We'll look after her, don't you worry. She'll be fine.'

I gave Aunty Gwen a goodbye pat. 'You get some sleep, Aunty. And don't worry, all right? I promise I'll go round first thing in the morning.'

She gave me a watery grin. 'What, me worry?'

I intercepted the nurse on my way out. 'She's, like, talking complete nonsense, you know? Keeps going on about visitors coming to her house, and she never, ever has any visitors.'

She shrugged. 'Well, that's concussion for you. The doctor will have another look at her tomorrow.'

'She thinks she'll be home tomorrow.'

'Oh, I doubt it, dear. She's old, and delayed shock can have all sorts of nasty effects on old people. I think she'll be in here a while yet.'

CHAPTER FOUR

I WENT to bed with my cup of cocoa, but couldn't sleep. I'd more or less put Aunty Gwen's 'visitor' down to her concussion, but for some reason I couldn't get the conversation out of my head. Was she feeding a stray cat or something? I couldn't leave some poor little kitty to starve, now, could I? I'd just have to bunk off school. Sigh. How sad. The mystery remained, but having come to a decision, I went to sleep.

Next morning: the usual breakfast battle between Ceri and Mam.

'At least have some cornflakes. Some muesli. A yoghurt.'

'No. You know I never eat breakfast. Stop going on at me all the time.'

'You'll be starving by eleven, and then you'll go and stuff chocolate, and that's empty calories; chocolate will give you zits and then you'll get fat and regret it.'

'Stop nagging! You're worse than toothache!'

'All the same, you know I'm right. Have a piece of toast.'

'Ceri, who's supposed to be the mam, you or me?'

'You. But somebody needs to take care of you.'

'Oh, for goodness' sake, Ceri!' And Mam slammed out.

See? Mad as a box of frogs under a full moon. They can't even get the nagging order right. Then Ceri left for work, muttering to herself, Dad folded his newspaper with a sigh (he wisely switches off completely in the mornings) and disappeared, and Steffan mooched off to call for his friend Cei. Which left *moi*, nicely alone and able to get up to bunking-off-school stuff. I changed out of my uniform and into jeans and a sweatshirt – and a bit of make-up for self-esteem, found an old towel, shoved it in a Tesco bag and headed off for Aunty's house. I stopped off at the corner shop for some cat food and got a funny look from Mrs Cadwallader.

'Is that cat food you're buying, Nia? Didn't know your family had a cat, then?'

Sigh. Why are grown-ups so nosy? I'd be as honest as the day is long if nobody asked awkward questions. 'Um!' I bleated, thinking fast on my feet. 'You're right. No cat! Um – collection in school for the NSPCC.'

'NSPCC? Little kids eating cat food these days, are they? I know times are hard, but –'

'Oh – did I say NSPCC? I meant the RSPCA.'

The CIA's got nothing on Mrs Cadwallader, trust me. She peered down her nose, one eye half shut, assessing me. Then her face changed. 'Oh, Nia, that reminds me – that nice Jamie Owen on the telly last night – not your Aunty Gwen who got attacked yesterday, was it? Even Derek mentioned it on the weather. Shocking, I call it! Was it your Gwenny?'

'Yeah. But she's OK.'

'She can't be OK if she's been beaten senseless!'

'She's OK, Mrs C. Bit shaken and bruised, but nothing serious.'

'Could turn nasty in a minute, at her age. Well, you give her my love, now, Nia; tell her if she wants anything urgent-like when they let her out, just get on the phone and I'll send our Idwal round with it.'

'I will, Mrs C. Thanks.' I took my cat food and scarpered before she could ask any more questions.

It wasn't a bad morning – the sun was shining, the birds were tweeting, and I wasn't in school. And, better still, who should amble round the corner but Rhyming Ryan O'Brien, jinking and weaving down the middle of the road. 'Ry?' I called, and he saw me and stopped.

'Hi-yaaah!' he said, squinting. 'What you doing out of school?'

'What are you?'

He grinned. 'Mitchin'. I hate science. I got no brains 'cept in my boots, so why bother, that's what I think. What about you?'

'I'm mitchin' too. My Aunty Gwen –'

'Oh, aye! Got mugged, she did, right?'

'Yeah. She'll be OK. But I've got to go and feed – well, I think it's a stray cat. Either that or she's totally lost it. She did have a bash on the head.'

'Shall I come?'

I wasn't saying no to the man of my dreams. 'Yeah. If you want to. Anyway,' I looked him up and down, 'if you're bunkin' off, what you wearing your uniform for?'

He pulled a face, and we started walking together. 'Couldn't help it, could I? Our mam don't work. Not like yours.'

'I'm not sure my mam actually *works*. She turns up at an office, yeah, but I don't think she does much. She's supposed to be a secretary, but she can only type about two words a minute.'

Ryan grinned. Then his face changed suddenly. 'Quick!' He grabbed my hoodie and dragged me backward into someone's front garden.

'Urgh!' I began, trying to choke quietly.

'It's the Kid Cops!' he hissed. 'Shurrup!'

The truancy patrol is the bane of our lives. They're Hobby Bobbies, special constables, and they drive an unmarked car and pounce on any kids that look like they ought to be in school. Not fair, to my way of thinking. Cheating, really. Mind, we all know the cars, but they can still sneak up on you if you don't keep an eye out. We hid behind the hedge until they'd cruised past.

When the car had turned the bend, we ran to the next corner and dived into another hedge. Sure enough, the sneaky so-and-sos drove round the block. See? They don't even play fair. At last they drove off towards the town centre, and it was a safe bet they wouldn't be back for at least half an hour. We'd be at Aunty Gwen's by then.

'I saw your Ceri down town yesterday afternoon,' Ryan said. 'I thought she was a real brain, but –'

'But? She is! She got A-stars in nearly everything!'

'Ah.' Ryan nodded. 'She going to uni, then?'

I sighed. 'She had offers from three, and her grades would have got her into any of them. But she says she wants to Be Free. Says she wants to experience the University of Life.' Yes, she honestly, really, truly said that. See what I mean about no common sense? University of Life is all very well, but it doesn't count for much on a job application form, does it?

'Oh, aye? So what's she doing?'

'She's at some employment agency. Lots of different short jobs. She says she couldn't bear to work in an office: she'd feel trapped.'

'Ah. That'd be why she was dressed up as a five-foot carrot, then, would it?'

'A *carrot*?' I started to laugh. 'Our Ceri?'

'Oh aye. Saw me, too, she did. Not over-pleased to see me, I could tell.'

I grinned. Oh, great! I'd have fun with this! We went round the back of Aunty Gwen's house. 'I'm going to have to break the window to get in,' I explained.

'Why?'

'Keys in her handbag, handbag got nicked, yeah?'

'Oh. Aye. Right.'

I found a big stone in the rockery, got the towel out of my carrier bag, wrapped it round the rock and my fist, and smashed the small windowpane in the back door. There. I bet you've been wondering about the towel, right? Now you know. When I had a hole big enough for my arm to go through, I felt around inside and undid the lock. The door swung open.

Aunty's house smelled stale and musty, although she'd only been away twenty-four hours. It wasn't a damp smell, or something gone bad, just strange. I opened a window to let in some fresh air, got out the cat food and rummaged in the kitchen drawer for a tin opener. Ryan, meanwhile, was wandering around, nosing.

I eventually found the tin opener on a hook by the stove and opened a can. Cat food's *disgusting*, all fishy and *bleaueww-ychafi*. Glad I'm not a cat. I looked round for a food dish with 'CAT' on it. There wasn't one. Then, out of the blue, I remembered what Aunty Gwen had said: 'Make some sandwiches. And there's a lamb bone.' Sandwiches? For a stray cat? Weird. Then I thought, *when I leave here, I'm going to lock the door and take the key. That's what Aunty said, right? So how is the visitor going to get in?* Aunty *was* concussed. I opened the fridge. There was the lamb bone. And a packet of plastic ham, the supermarket sort that doesn't taste of anything. There was Wondabred in the bread bin, so I sighed and made a couple of sarnies and wrapped them in cling film, got the lamb bone out, scraped the cat food onto a saucer and sighed. 'That's it,' I said. 'We can go now. Ryan? Where are you?'

He was in the front room. 'This is, like, dead weird.'

'What?' I wandered in. He was staring at a photo. I went and stood beside him. He was wearing some sort of aftershave. It smelled nice, not tear-gassy and stinky like the cheap stuff.

'Look at him.'

'What about him?'

'Well, look – he's in a couple of the pictures, see? The other people's clothes change – sometimes they're wrapped up warm, sometimes they're in light clothes – but his don't. He's always wearing the same stuff.'

I peered at the photos: I don't think I'd ever looked at them before, not properly. Some of them were in black and white, showing a very young Aunty Gwen, with two ladies I didn't know, and then there was this figure in the middle. It was so muffled up with hat, scarf, overcoat and sunglasses, you couldn't be sure if it was a bloke or not, although the clothes looked like men's clothes.

'And there's this one too,' Ryan went on, pointing to another wall. 'Look, it's the same bloke, looking exactly the same!'

He was right. The person was in other photos, too, in just the same scarf and hat; although the others in the picture might be in summer dresses, short-sleeved shirts, whatever – the weirdo was always muffled up.

'I'll ask Aunty Gwen when she comes home,' I decided.

Ryan made his voice all spooky. '*Maybeeee* – it's the *Invisible Maaaan*. Beneath those bandages there's –'

'*Nooooooothiiiiing!*' I finished, and laughed.

'Anyway, we can go now. It's prob'ly been a wasted effort, but at least when I visit Aunty Gwen I can look her in the eye and tell her I did what she asked, right?'

'Right,' agreed Ryan.

I found a bit of cardboard and wedged it in the broken window and closed the shutters too. They wouldn't keep a determined burglar out, but it should be all right. This was a quiet area, and there wasn't much crime. The house should be safe enough.

Outside, we stood awkwardly on the pavement.

'What we going to do now, then?' Ryan asked.

I looked at my watch. 'Science is over. What's this afternoon?'

He suddenly looked horrified. 'Oooh Myyyy Gaaaard! Games! It's rugby!'

I rolled my eyes. 'Like, so?'

'*Sooo?* What d'you mean, like, soooo?'

'Yeah. So you miss rugby. What's the big deal?'

'Torturer Tim said that anyone who misses games today won't get on the team.'

Oh, how awful. Not. I am not the athletic type. 'So – what will you do?'

'Go to school, what else? I'll tell 'im I was bad in bed this morning. Got to go, Ni! I got to get on the team!'

I sighed. 'All right. See you.'

'Tomorrow, yeah?'

'Oh – yeah.' I tried to remember my Friday timetable. Oh, yes. English, history – and art. All subjects I enjoyed. 'See you in school. And, Ryan?'

'Yeah?' He was already sprinting down the road, and turned to look at me, running backwards.

'Hope you get on the team, Ry!'

CHAPTER FIVE

No point in going to school just yet. Back home for a bit of lunch, and then in for the afternoon. I made beans on toast and ate at the kitchen table, washed up the stuff and put it away after. Dirty dishes in the sink would have been a dead giveaway.

I needn't have bothered. I was upstairs, putting on my, like, totally disgusting school shirt (bottle-green aertex polo with a purple and green badge) when I heard the front door open. *Swearword!* I thought. The front door slammed, and I peeked over the banisters. Ceri. Oh, rats. Maybe I could lurk upstairs until she'd had lunch and gone back to work. I lay on my bed and waited. And waited. If she didn't go soon, I'd be late for art.

At ten to one she was still downstairs, slamming about in the kitchen. Maybe I could sneak out without her seeing me. Carrying my shoes, I crossed the landing, tiptoed down the stairs and into the hall. I had my hand on the door latch. I was *so nearly out of there . . .*

'Nia? What are you doing home?'

'I – um – forgot my art apron.'

'No you didn't. You keep it in school! You bunked off, didn't you!'

It wasn't a question. 'What if I have? None of your business, is it?'

'Oh yes it is,' she said, prissily. 'What sort of exam results will you get if you're never in school?'

'As good as yours, any day,' I retorted. 'And if I get straight A-stars, I certainly won't waste them dressing up as a fat carrot!'

She froze. 'What?'

'Ryan O'Brien saw you. You were being a carrot.'

'Did he say *fat carrot*?'

'No. Just *carrot*.'

'So it's you calling me fat, is it?'

'Who, me? Would I do that?'

'Yes, you would! I'm telling Dad you bunked off.'

'And I'll tell everyone you spend your days dressed up as a carrot!'

'You wouldn't!'

'I would.'

Then my big, tough sister burst into tears, and I felt awful. 'Aw, don't cry, Ceri – I won't tell anyone.'

'I don't care.' Her voice was snotty and muffled.

'Yes, you do, or you wouldn't be crying.'

'It's not the carrot thing I'm crying about. It's worse.'

'What? A banana or a brussels sprout tomorrow?'

'Oh, ha ha. Very funny. Not.' She blew her nose and sniffed. 'It's awful. I've been spotted.'

'What do you mean, spotted? Someone saw you being a carrot? I thought you said –'

'Spotted as in talent-spotted. I've got a part in a TV show.'

'Oh yeah? Pull the other one, Ceri; it's got bells on.'

'No, honest. I was sitting in the Coffi Caffi drinking a skinny *latte* –'

'Instant with skim milk, you mean?'

'Shut up and listen. This bloke came in, and ordered a meat pie and chips, and he was, like, watching me the whole time. It was really embarrassing, Ni.'

'Yeah, right. What *was* he after, do you think?' I said.

'I was getting my stuff together to go back to work when he came over and shoved this in my hand.' She rummaged in her bag and brought out a small blue card: ***SuperTalent Inc. Maldwyn Verdun Goldwyn-Jones**, **Entrepreneur**.* And a Cardiff address on the back.

'And you, like, believe this, do you? What planet you from, Cer?'

'But it's for real! That's why I'm home now. I took a morning off work –'

'– from being a carrot –'

'Shut up and listen. I went to Cardiff, Saturday, and found the office and, Ni, it's, like, really posh! It's got glass doors and plastic plants and a secretary and everything! And photos on the wall of him with people like Matthew Rhys and Brad Pitt!'

I sighed. 'Things like that can be faked, Cer! So easily.'

'You can sneer, Nia, but I had an audition at the TV studios this morning. Ni – I'm going to be on telly! *Curse of the Full Moon*. It's a series and I'm going to be in three whole episodes. Acting!'

'But – you can't!'

'Yes, I can, Ni! I got the sixth-form drama prize, didn't I? Mr Goldwyn-Jones is gonna sort out an Equity card and everything!'

'But –' From her expression, she'd tear me limb from

limb if I said anything sarky. So I didn't, not because I was afraid, but because I'd been hit with a Horrible Thought. 'But what about Mam?' I whispered.

'Exactly!' my sister wailed. 'What about Mam?'

I forgot all about going to school and sat down on the bottom step of the stairs. 'Oh, sh . . . oot, Ceri! There's gonna be hell to pay when she finds out!'

'What am I going to do? I'll have to back out, won't I? She'd never forgive me if I got famous and she didn't! What can I do, Nia? I can't do it, can I?'

I chewed my thumbnail and thought. I pictured my poor, stage-struck mam, who was never, ever going to make it as an actress, no matter how hard she tried and how many auditions she went to. How would she take finding out that Ceri was going to be one, and by accident, too, because she'd met a bloke in a caff?

'I can't do it, Nia, can I?' she said again, looking like she'd be in floods any minute.

'What, and spend the rest of your life being a fat carrot? I don't think so! There must be some way –'

She must have been really upset, because she ignored the 'fat'. 'You think of one, then.'

I chewed my nail some more, and spat a bit out. 'We could just – not tell her.'

'How long do you think I'd get away with that?'

'Well, think about it, Cer. If you do make this telly programme . . . Is it definite?'

'Yeah. It's been commissioned, so it's already sold.'

'Oh. Well, no need for her to know anything until it's actually going to be on, and then we just won't tell her. The night it's on, we'll – we'll – we'll take her out somewhere so she can't possibly see it!'

'And nobody else in the world sees it either, I suppose? There are no repeats and it's not available on iPlayer?'

'No, loads of people will see it – but then she'll be really proud of you, and she won't mind so much.'

Ceri gave me a doubtful look. 'You think?'

I thought about it. 'No. Not really. She'll be spitting blood and chewing carpets.'

'I'll have to say I can't do it, won't I, Nia?'

'No! You can't! Mam's going to have to live with it. She just can't act and everybody knows it. It's only her who doesn't! Even when she was playing a dead person on a stretcher she was terrible. You've got to go for it, Ceri. We'll keep it a secret until we can't any more, and then we'll tell her. She'll have to like it or lump it.'

'You think it'll work?'

'Yes. It has to, because you can't pass up a chance like this. Do you want to go on being a carrot all your life?'

'No.'

'Then you've got to go for it, right?'

My big sister looked determined. 'Promise you won't tell anyone, Nia?'

'Cross my heart. Can I ask you something?'

'Anything. You're a good kid, Nia –'

'I know. I'm the best. Why were you being a fat carrot?'

'– but I'll kill you if you mention carrots again. Anyway, gotta go. I'm doing a demonstration of automatic tomato slicers this afternoon.'

I was late for afternoon registration. I got a right

rollicking from the head of year, and another from Mrs Richards art, who accused me of 'wasting my talent' and 'letting myself down' and all the other stuff that adults lay on kids when they want to hit you with a guilt trip. I did some more work on my collage, and then went home at half past three, waving at Ryan who didn't see me because he was charging shoulder first into a scrummage machine with his bum in the air.

Steffan was sitting on the doorstep making intergalactic battle sounds, so I let him into the house. He dropped his school bag and rugby kit on the floor and charged upstairs, making a *sheeeeaaaaoooooeeouw* noise, like Superman leaping a tall building at a single bound. I started laying the table and peeling spuds for tea. I wondered if we'd all go and see Aunty Gwen in hospital tonight, or just some of us. I looked in the fridge, hoping to see something, anything, that might make an evening meal, but there was only an out-of-date rhubarb yoghurt and half a tin of spaghetti hoops that had gone black around the inside of the tin. I got a couple of cans of corned beef out of the larder and put them in the fridge so the meat would be easy to slice. Corned beef and chips – not exactly Jamie Oliver, but better than nothing if you're hungry.

Steffan thudded downstairs, wearing an ancient knitted balaclava that was too big for him. 'What's for tea, Nia?' he asked, somewhat muffled by navy wool.

'Corned beef and chips. Who's asking?'

He adjusted his balaclava and peered at me through the eyeholes. 'Hatman!'

'Hatman?'

'Yeah. I get special powers from my hat. This hat makes

me invisible, an' I can climb up the outside of houses with my suckin' fingers an' blast people with my X-ray stare.'

'Right. Got any homework?'

He pulled himself up to his full height. 'Hatman don't do no steenkin' 'omework!' he hissed.

'Mexican superhero, Hatman, is he?'

'Of course not, stupid! He's – he's a Welsh superhero!'

'I see. Eats leeks and daffodils for his superhuman strength, yeah?'

My little brother turned red with fury, tore off his balaclava and rushed upstairs wailing: 'I hate you, Nia! I'm gonna get you for that, you rotten moo! I'm gonna run away an' it'll be all your fault!'

'I'll make you some sandwiches, then,' I shouted after him. 'What do you want, corned beef or cheese?'

'Shut up, you fat, you fat *fooomph*!' I think he thought he was swearing.

Dad came in then, closely followed by Ceri, who mouthed, 'Not one word, right?' I winked.

Mam was late. Very late. I'd chopped the chips, put the chip pan on and sliced the corned beef, and we were all sitting round with rumbling tummies when the phone went. Dad sighed and answered it. 'Oh. Right. We'll start without you, then. See you later, love.'

He came in and sat down. 'That was your mam. She's been to Cardiff, and she's going to stop off to see Gwen on her way home. She'll pick up a Chinese for herself, so we can go ahead and eat.'

'Hooray,' Steffan muttered. 'I haven't eaten f'rages. I could die of starvation and nobody'd notice.'

'Yes, we would,' Ceri assured him, rummaging in the cupboard for pickle. 'There wouldn't be any irritating little brats rushing round the house making weird noises.'

Steffan stuck out his tongue. 'One day, when I'm a world-famous superhero, you'll be sorry you were horrible to me, Ceri.'

You know how, sometimes, you can completely forget to do something? And then suddenly right out of the blue you remember it? I was sitting there, waiting to start my food, when I saw myself locking Aunty Gwen's back door, and – leaving the key in the lock.

Oh – shoot! I leapt up and ran to my hoodie to feel in the pockets. Rats. I was going to have to go back and get the key when I'd had my tea. I couldn't leave it sticking out of the lock, even in a safe area like this, could I?

CHAPTER SIX

M Y TURN to stack the dishwasher. I did it quickly, then scarpered. For late September, the weather was amazing, and the sun was still out. From the top of the hill near Aunty Gwen's house I could see it sitting on the horizon like a fat red beach ball, a ghostly moon alongside getting ready for the night shift.

I turned down the back lane and opened the gate in the wall, trotted up to the back door – and to my relief found the key still in the lock, so no one had spotted it, thank goodness. I made sure the door was locked and put the key in my pocket. I was just about to leave when I heard a noise inside the house. Aunty Gwen, out of hospital already? Surely she'd have phoned and told us? Better check. I got the key out again and opened the back door. No one in the kitchen. I looked in the little-old-lady-brown living room, and in the dining room that overlooked the garden, then went to the foot of the stairs.

'Aunty Gwen?' I called. 'Are you there?'

The house suddenly went utterly silent, and then there was a quick, light, scuffling, scratching sound from behind the cellar door. I froze, and my brain sort of went into reverse. *There was something in the cellar! Or someone!*

Then I suddenly thought *ohgoodgrief!* Aunty Gwen was mugged, her handbag stolen. Her house keys and her wallet

– complete with address no doubt – had been in her bag. I reached into my jeans pocket for my mobile, but then I remembered I'd put it on charge before I came out. Now I was going to get mugged and murdered, and all because of a flat battery. The nearest phone was Aunty Gwen's, but any self-respecting criminals would have cut the wires, wouldn't they? And if I went to use it, I'd get caught, no question. There was a phone box a couple of hundred metres down the road – but by the time I got there the intruders would probably be long gone.

Then, quite suddenly, I wasn't scared any more (well, a bit – but 'angry' quite unexpectedly took over from 'terrified'). I looked around for a weapon. There was an umbrella stand in the hall with a broken blue umbrella in it – and my late Uncle Caradog's golf clubs that Aunty Gwen couldn't bear to part with. I selected the putter, eased open the cellar door, the club poised to strike, and crept down the stairs. Suddenly I remembered seeing the kitchen table – the sandwiches and lamb bone I'd left out had gone! Now *that* made me really mad. The rotten muggers had even eaten Aunty Gwen's plastic ham! How dared they?

I hadn't, of course, put the cellar light on – that would have been dumb even for me – and it was really, really dark down there. The only window was the small, dirt-encrusted pane in the basement door, and any light would have crept half a metre in and then died from exhaustion – and outside it was getting dark anyway. The house was quite old, and the cellar was the oldest part of it, because a newer house had been built about a hundred years ago, on top of the foundations of an older one. The cellar walls were supported by heavy oak beams that were much, much older. A dendrochronologist (that's my one and only thousand-pound word – it means one of those blokes on *Time Team* who can tell the age of wood by counting tree rings or something) could have dated it, I expect. But the beams made nasty, dark, shadowy recesses, and I'd started to shake. I waited on the bottom step, my golf club poised, ready to batter the living daylights out of anything that so much as twitched. I held my breath and listened. Everything was absolutely silent.

If this had been in a film, there would have been loads of 'da-da-da-da-da-da-dummmmmm' music on the soundtrack. Then the blonde American film star with the golf club would have been leapt upon and done for by the knife-wielding homicidal maniac, accompanied by lots of 'scrraaaaaa-scraaaa-scraaaa' music. But I'm not blonde or a film star and I'm Welsh, and I meant business. My free hand fumbled around to where I knew there was a light switch . . .

'Please don't put the light on!'

You know that feeling when your whole insides sort of lurch when you're really scared? 'Who's that? Where are you? Come out at once!'

'I – can't.'

'What do you mean, you can't? Come out now, or else! I've called the police!' I lied. 'They'll be here any minute now. And don't think you can mug me like you mugged my Aunty Gwen. I'm not old and I'm armed.'

'Yes. I know. I can see you.'

How? I couldn't see a thing. The cellar was black as a mole's left nostril.

'Have you got those infra-red glasses?'

'No. I – I just have excellent eyesight. I think you should go away now. Please?'

'I'm not going anywhere, mate. Come on out, right now, or I'm coming after you!'

'Oh, please don't! Please, just go away?'

It was a panicky sort of voice, and sounded about my own age and a bit uncertain. It didn't sound like a tough, scary sort of mugger's voice, not one bit. And it was only one voice, not two. Quite suddenly, I stopped being scared. My fingers groped for the light switch. I flicked it, squinting in the sudden brightness.

Standing in the corner of Aunty Gwen's old cellar, also squinting, was a boy of about my own age.

A tall boy.

A very worried-looking boy. Dressed in the oddest collection of clothes I'd ever seen on a kid my age – a pair of khaki shorts which ended just above his knees, one of those knitted V-necked sleeveless pullovers that are all mad patterns, and a sick-green shirt with a weirdly long collar.

'What are you doing in my aunty's cellar?' I shrieked. 'You mugger!'

'Don't shout, don't shout! It hurts my ears!'

'Tough!' I screamed even louder. 'Serves you right for mugging my aunty and breaking in!'

'I didn't, I didn't!' The boy started towards me.

'Don't come near me! Stay where you are, or else!'

'Oh, please, I won't hurt you. I promise!'

'Yeah, right. Just like you didn't hurt Aunty Gwen. You deserve to be beaten to death with this golf club! She's an old lady; she could have died. What have you done with her pension money, you rotten, stinking mugger, you?'

His face was red and he looked panic-stricken. 'I haven't got her money! I didn't –'

'Spent it already, have you?'

'No! And I'd never hurt Gwen! She's kind. She's my friend; I wouldn't hurt her, I swear. I don't know who robbed her, but if I ever find out, I'll –'

'I don't believe you!' I bellowed.

His hands went over his ears again. 'Please, please, *please stop shouting! I can't stand it. It hurts.*'

I was starting to calm down now. 'Look. If you aren't a mugger, then who are you? What are you doing in my aunty's cellar? And where did you get those terrible clothes?'

The boy glanced despairingly over his shoulder, through the filthy glass of the cellar door. 'I sort of live here. Aunty Gwen lets me stay. She lent me the clothes. They belonged to her husband, I think.'

I lowered the golf club. 'Let me get this straight. You *live in Aunty Gwen's cellar?*'

He nodded. He was quite nice-looking, if a bit scruffy. I suppose clothes my dead uncle probably wore in the seventies would do that to a bloke. He was tall – probably over six feet, with a mass of thick dark hair and bright eyes that slanted slightly upward at the corners. 'I've lived here for years. I don't always stay in the cellar, mind – sometimes I come upstairs and sit with her, if she's on her own.'

'You can't have lived here for years! Aunty Gwen would have said something. How old are you?'

'Fifteen.'

Close to my age, then. 'So, you're sort of a lodger.'

He shrugged. 'Sort of.'

'What do you mean, sort of?'

'I mean, yes, I suppose I am.'

'Let me get this straight. You're my age, and you're living with my aunty. And she never mentioned it. What about your parents? They chuck you out?'

'No. I ran away.'

'So you sponge off Aunty Gwen, I suppose?'

'I don't. Gwen feeds me, yes. She's kind, your aunty. I don't know what I'd do without her. She's wonderful. But in return I help her as much as I can. I do the gardening for her sometimes, and I help her clean the house and stuff.'

'So why didn't she mention you?'

'I made her promise not to.'

'Why? We – her family, I mean – we wouldn't have minded!'

He picked at the edge of the ghastly pullover with his fingernails.

'Well, now *I* know about you, you'd better come upstairs, I suppose. You first!' I didn't want him behind me. I still had my golf club ready if he tried anything.

I herded him into the living room, where the last bits of sunshine tinted the picture rail. 'Right, sit down,' I ordered, and meekly, he did, gazing up at me. His eyes really were extraordinary. As well as the slight upwards slant, the eyelashes were thick and dark, and his irises were clear golden-brown. Beautiful eyes that would have looked really great on me, since my eyes disappear entirely without a bit of make-up.

'Tell me everything,' I said, perching on the settee arm opposite him, still clutching my weapon. I was ready to wallop him if he so much as twitched in my direction.

The boy glanced out of the window. The sun had nearly gone and the moon was brightening. 'Please, will you go now?' he asked. His voice sounded sort of desperate. 'Please? You really should go home.'

'What, so you can make a run for it?'

'No. But you shouldn't be here. It's getting dark outside.'

'I'm not scared.'

'You shouldn't be out on your own at night!' He was almost shouting, now.

'Why? What are you so worried about?'

He closed his eyes. 'You wouldn't understand.'

I didn't quite know what to make of him. Something inside me was sort of warming to him. He actually seemed pretty harmless, but his tone of voice, his insistence that I got home before dark, now *they* were beginning to scare me! 'I don't understand what all the fuss is about. There are street lamps, and loads of people about and anyway there's going to be a lovely big, bright moon!'

He was fidgeting nervously, glancing through the window into the dusk outside.

'What's the matter with you?'

'You must –'

And then we heard the noise.

CHAPTER SEVEN

I SHUSHED him with a finger on my lips, crept to the door and peeked out. A shadow moved on the other side of the stained-glass panel in the front door. A key scraped at the lock. Whoever it was was tall – so it wasn't Aunty Gwen, who's five-foot-nothing and egg-shaped. I shot back into the living room. 'I think it's one of the muggers!' I whispered. 'Aunty Gwen's keys were in her handbag! Come on – let's sort him out. We'll teach him not to mug little old ladies!'

But he grabbed my hand, towed me into the kitchen, opened the cellar door and hauled me through it. He tugged me down a couple of steps and shut the door behind us. 'What are you doing?' I whispered into the darkness. 'We can get him! Make a citizen's arrest! Call the police and tell them we've caught a burglar!' Who was I kidding? 'Or we can just bash him as hard as we can and then call the police to come and get what's left!' I liked that idea much better, especially the bashing part.

He said nothing. Maybe he was the strong, silent type. 'Come on. Help me!' I hissed, urgently. Still no answer. I felt around in the darkness, but couldn't find him. 'Where are you?'

'Down here.'

'Where?'

The sun had set, but the moon was out, and shining in – just – through the filthy glass in the cellar door. I could barely see the shadowy figure at the bottom of the steps. 'Oh, come on, *please*! We can do it together! I'll clobber him with the golf club, and you can tackle him and sit on him. Then we'll tie him up and phone the police.'

No answer. 'You rotten wimp!' I said disgustedly. 'Are you going to let me tackle him all by myself?'

He muttered something back at me, but I didn't understand it. I could hear him moving about at the bottom of the stairs. Probably trying to hide somewhere. Honestly, how can people be such cowards?

'Right,' I hissed. I crept up the steps and opened the cellar door a crack. 'Up to me, then. Thanks for your help, chum. Aunty Gwen will be proud of you. Not.' Trust me to get landed with a total wuss when what I needed was a Superhero! Even Hatman might do . . .

My golf club at the ready, I eased open the cellar door, stepped into the kitchen and crept along the hall. I could hear drawers being opened and closed in the living room, and clinking noises as the mugger rifled Aunty's sideboard cupboards. Uncle Caradog's putter raised, I crept through the door.

A guy of about twenty, scruffy hoodie and baggy trousers drooping down and showing his pants, and thick-soled trainers with the laces tucked into the tops, was inspecting Aunty's sideboard clock. He dropped it on the floor and picked up a little silver and glass bumble-bee jam pot I'd loved since I was little. No way was he having that!

I crept forward, prepared to give him an almighty whack. I'd show him! Then, suddenly, the club was wrenched backwards and a rough hand grabbed my wrist from behind. I shrieked, and turned.

'That's not nice, now, is it?' the new arrival said. He was smirking, holding the club out of my reach while I struggled to get away. 'You can't go around hitting people – that's not friendly. We never done you no harm. No call for violence, love.' He sniggered.

'And what's mugging old ladies, then? Care in the community?' I panted, trying to kick his shins. He held me off easily, being much bigger than me. He had pasty skin, squinty blue eyes and gingery hair, what little of it I could see under his black baseball cap. It was beginning to dawn on me that I might just possibly be in real trouble. There were two of them against just me, since my brave companion was hiding in the cellar! I fought and kicked and tried to bite, but the boy was holding me too firmly and I was trapped. Then the other one joined in, wrapping his arm round my neck, half choking me. I hauled at his arm, desperately trying to pull it away from my throat. The one holding my other arm let go and stood back.

'Interfering little thing, aren't you?' he sniggered. 'What shall we do with her, Dwayne?' He tossed the golf club on the floor.

Dwayne sniffed and scraped lank hair out of his eyes. 'Oooh, now, let me see,' he said. 'I'm sure we can think of something. We got a nice, quiet house in a nice, quiet neighbourhood – and there's two of us and one of her.'

I opened my mouth and let out a shriek. Not one of my

best. I've done louder when I've been fighting with Ceri. If I wanted the neighbours to hear me, I'd have to do better than that. The one holding my neck clapped his free hand across my mouth. His hand smelled of stale cigarettes. I bit him anyway, sank my teeth in and really hung on. I didn't care about germs. He yelled and shook me off, so I was free at last, but the other one grabbed at me as I made a frantic dash for the door.

'Heeeeelp!' I shrieked at the top of my voice. 'You let me go, you pigs! I'm telling the police as soon as I get out of here. I know your faces now! I can identify you! You won't get away with this!' Which was possibly the dumbest thing I'd said all day, I realised, the instant the words were out of my mouth. So I just let out another shriek and kicked and struggled a lot.

They were both holding me now, and Dwayne used his free hand to land me a good wallop. A punch, not a slap. I saw stars and sagged, eyes shut, holding my aching cheek.

Then I heard a strange noise. It was my day for strange noises. It sounded like a growl. Nah. I was hearing things. Aunty Gwen didn't have a dog. Just a totally useless lodger. Dwayne let go of me, suddenly, and then the other one did. I crumpled onto my knees, feeling sick and dizzy. Then I waited . . . and waited.

I opened one eye. My captors were staring at something behind me, their mouths open. They started to back away, slowly at first, then faster, then they both turned and ran for it. Trying to get out, they got stuck side by side in the hall doorway, then burst free, their flapping shoelaces clicking on the tiled floor. I heard them wrench open the front door, and then I heard the wonderful sound of feet pounding down the path.

Something had scared them. I was grateful for that – but I wasn't entirely sure I wanted to turn round and look at what it was. But I did. In the kitchen doorway was the biggest dog I have ever seen in my life. From where I was crouching on the living-room floor, I was actually looking up at it. It looked like a cross between an Alsatian, a Rottweiler and a Tyrannosaurus rex. The fur around its neck bristled, its head was lowered, the eyes half-closed, and the lips were drawn back from a set of choppers that looked to have been individually sharpened. I thought I might possibly be eaten alive in the next ten seconds.

It wasn't even looking at me. In fact it totally ignored me, padded past me into the hall, claws clicking on the tiles just as shoelaces had moments earlier. Then there was silence. I got up, slowly, and went to the door. The hall was empty. The front door gaped open onto the moonlit street.

The dog was gone. And so were the muggers. I didn't waste any time closing and locking the front door. When Aunty Gwen came out of hospital I'd find out who that big, beautiful, wonderful hound belonged to, and buy it the biggest, meatiest bone I could find. It never even occurred to me to wonder how it had got into the house.

I was shaking all over, my teeth chattering with delayed fright. My heart was going about ten times faster than usual, and I felt a bit weepy, if I'm honest. That, I thought, would be the effects of the adrenalin in my system, which proves that I probably watch too much *Casualty*. And I was stressed. So

I had a bit of a 'really feeling quite sorry for myself' cry and felt a lot better.

I collected the front-door keys from the sideboard where the muggers had thrown them, locked the back door from the inside and let myself – cautiously – out through the front. There were no signs of either muggers or dog.

I debated whether to stop off at the cop shop on the way home, and report Dwayne and his mate but, if I did, the police would probably insist on taking me home in a police car afterwards. I hoped Dwayne and the Ginger Squinty Person might have lost some of their enthusiasm for creeping round empty houses, if not for mugging old ladies. Besides, I only had the name, Dwayne, and that wouldn't take the police very far, would it? No, better let sleeping dogs lie!

I walked home through the darkening streets, feeling scared for the first time ever on my home turf. This was little more than a village, not quite a town. I'd gone to Brownies alone when I was seven, taken myself to and from school every day – no problem – but now I'd been badly scared, and I didn't like the feeling one bit. I jumped at every shadow, crossed the road if I saw someone walking towards me, and once, when I heard footsteps echoing behind me, I picked up my heels and ran hell-for-leather towards home. I was *scared*.

And as for that weird boy, if I ever saw him again I'd have a few words to say. Even if he was a bit short in the brain department, he had no right to go off and leave me on my own with two criminals. He might at least have backed me up when I needed it; he was big enough and ugly enough, and he hadn't exactly looked *weedy*. Thank goodness for

Wonderdog! Without its help, I could have ended up a crime statistic! I felt, like, totally traumatised!

Suddenly I stopped feeling terrified and started grinding my teeth. I wasn't going to let them get away with this. I'd get them somehow if it was the last thing I did, not because of roughing me up, but because of what they did to Aunty Gwen. Sooner or later, I'd have 'em.

I was so glad to get home. I pushed open the back door and went in. Mam's jacket was slung on the kitchen table, and her handbag was spilling junk out everywhere, so I sighed, hung the jacket tidily on the back of a chair, and then started to pick up the stuff from her handbag and put it back.

Among the crumpled tissues, lipsticks, purses and leaky biros was a familiar-looking, small blue business card . . .

Coincidence? Or did Mr Maldwyn Verdun Goldwyn-Jones now have *two* members of my family on his books? Now that would be a complication I could do without.

CHAPTER EIGHT

I SHOVED the card back in Mam's bag and zipped it shut. I had that feeling in the region of my belly button that told me that something was Horribly Wrong. The telly wasn't on in the living room. That was scary: it's *always* on when Mam's home, because she likes to criticise all the actors, like she could do that part *so much* better. But tonight, no telly. Instead, Mam, Dad, Ceri and Steffan sitting in a circle, staring at each other. Mam's face was pink, and her eyes were shining.

'What's up?' I asked, flopping onto the sofa beside Ceri.

'Where have you been?' Mam asked. 'We've all been waiting for you.'

'I've –' I began, but she didn't wait for an answer.

'I've got something really exciting to tell you.' She was twisting her hands together and breathing deeply. Oh crumbs. Bad sign, that, with Mam. Ceri shot a panicky glance at me. I raised my right eyebrow (I've been practising doing that). Steffan pulled his balaclava down so it covered his eyes. Hatman was alive and well and living in Cwmdaran Street, but he knew when to opt out.

Mam bit her lip and looked down at her hands. No point in trying to hurry her: in this mood, she'd speak when she was ready, and not before.

At last. 'You were all so sure I couldn't do it, weren't you!' (This was a statement, not a question.) 'Well, I've proved you all wrong. I've done it.'

'Oh, good grief,' Dad said impatiently. 'What have you done, exactly? Just tell us and get it over with, will you? I want to watch the rugby!'

'I,' she said slowly, 'have got a part in a television drama. I've resigned my job at the estate agent's and I'm going to be an actress.'

Ceri's eyes got very wide, and so did her mouth. I dug her in the ribs. *'Shuttup!'* I whispered.

'And what,' my hopeless mam said happily, 'do you think of that?'

'Oh,' we all said together.

'Oh? Is that all?'

'Congratulations, Mam,' I said, and the others chimed in. Ceri was beaming. She thought she was off the hook because Mam had an acting job, so she wouldn't care so much if Ceri had one too. But I had a sneaky, sinking feeling that this was all just beginning. Had I been a seafaring sort of person, I would have seen rocks ahead. Big, fat, nasty, jagged ones that were about to tear the bottom out of poor Ceri's little boat and sink her to the bottom of the deep blue sea.

'Yeah, great, Mam. F'ntastic. Can we watch the rugby now?' Hatman hauled up his eyeholes and peered out.

Mam sighed. 'Don't you want to know all about my big break?'

'Oh. Yes, love. Course we do,' my dad said, picking up the telly zapper and pointing it at the box.

Mam glared. 'Are you *really* going to put that on? When I've just told you my news? My night of triumph and not one of you is remotely interested! My own family and you couldn't care less! Oh, I'm going to bed!'

She flounced upstairs, and Dad clicked on the goggle box, where a commentator was going off on one about the Cardiff Blues.

'Isn't it great?' Ceri whispered, her eyes shining. 'I'm off the hook, and I've been *so worried* all day!'

Inside, I groaned. I was going to have to burst my sister's happybubble. 'We need to talk, Cer,' I muttered. 'Come into the kitchen.'

She followed me and put the kettle on for tea. She was still grinning like an idiot. 'What you looking so down about, Nia? You've got a face like a slapped backside!'

'So will yours be in a minute. Look, Ceri, you're not off the hook at all.'

'But I *am*! She won't care two hoots about what I do if she's got a part in something! Wonder what it is?'

Silently, I opened Mam's handbag, fished out the little blue card and handed it to her.

'Where'd she get that? It was in my –' Her eyes went big with shock. 'Oh, no! It's hers, isn't it?'

I nodded. 'I think Maldwyn Verdun wossname might have talent-spotted her, too.' Didn't say much about his abilities, mind, did it? Not if he'd 'spotted' Mam! Unless she'd seen his ad somewhere and gone to see him. 'Ceri, what if she's got a part in the same thing you're in? And if she's only an extra –'

'Which is likely, because she certainly can't act.'

'Exactly – then she finds out about you. How big is your part anyway?'

She slumped into a kitchen chair. 'Pretty big. I'm the second lead, the attractive psychological profiler who helps the dishy detective to solve all the crimes. Oh hell. Lots of dead bodies, all the senior officers are baffled and we go and solve it. Me and the dishy detective. So –'

I was ahead of her. If there was a dead body, bet your bottom dollar Mam was it. And when she found out Ceri was playing second lead, she was not going to be a happy bunny, was she?

'Oh, why couldn't we have a normal mam, Nia?' Ceri wailed. 'A help-out-in-school-and-cake-baking mam? Where did we go wrong? D'you think it's karma? We did something terrible in a past life and this family is our punishment?'

'I'm normal,' I said. 'Not sure about you, though. Come on.' I patted her arm. 'I'll make us a cuppa and we'll go and watch Dad watching the rugby. That's always good for a laugh. And don't worry. At least you *know* about Mam now, so it won't come as a shock when you start rehearsals. And at least you don't have to be a carrot any more. Maybe something will turn up. There's light at the end of the tunnel.'

Ceri sighed. 'The trouble with lights at the end of tunnels –'

I finished it for her: '– is that it might just be the Paddington to Swansea express bearing down on you.'

'Yeah,' she said gloomily.

I poured the water onto the teabags and rummaged for some biscuits in the tin.

'Oh – I nearly forgot, Ni. Aunty Gwen will be out of hospital tomorrow, so we don't have to go in and see her.'

That was good. I wanted a long chat, alone, with Aunty!

Next morning Mam was bit miffed and distant, but she trotted off to work out her notice at the estate agent's office in Stryd Fawr. I hoped they'd take her back when her acting career was over. Which it would be. Probably very soon.

I like Fridays in school: for a start, there's that lovely weekend-here-I-come feeling; and we finish at three instead of half past because we have a short lunchtime. On Fridays we get proper lessons in the morning and in the afternoon we get to choose what we do. For me this means art.

That day I did loads of work, and Mrs Richards was dead impressed. 'If only you were as enthusiastic about English and maths as you are about art, Nia,' she sighed. 'I'd like to see you get some really good exam results and eventually get into a top-class university.'

'I can get into college with just art,' I muttered. 'Pentre Gwaelod.' I know when the staff have been talking about me; I'm not daft. Especially with the dreaded Parents' Evening looming on the horizon.

'I'm going to tell you, Nia, although I probably shouldn't,' Mrs Richards said quietly, 'but some of the staff believe that you should be banned from art until you're up to date with your other work. You're an extremely able girl. Your written English is excellent when you bother, you're an avid reader, and while your maths isn't brilliant, it's not hopeless either. You could do outstandingly well. Why can't you understand that your future begins now?'

Sigh. 'Yes, Mrs Richards.' The horrible thing was, I knew she was right. I'd have to get on with some revision and work harder and stop missing school if I wanted to get any qualifications, let alone good ones.

When the last bell rang, Ryan dashed up, sweaty in his rugby kit, his ears strapped down with Elastoplast and his eyebrows thick with Vaseline. Not a pretty sight. 'See you tomorrow, then? 'Bout one o'clock? Kick-off's two-thirty – we'll grab a hot dog first. Orright?'

'Yeah. Orright. See you, Ryan.'

He loped off towards the pitch, one sock up, one down, his hairy legs smeared with mud.

I decided to pop in to see Aunty Gwen on the way home. She should be out of hospital by now, and I wanted to make sure she was all right. And have a Talk with her, too. Find out all about That Boy.

I still had her front-door key, so I let myself in, calling out: 'Aunty Gwen? You there?' No answer. I went into the living room, but she wasn't there, nor was she upstairs, although I looked in all three bedrooms. Perhaps the hospital hadn't let her out yet. I checked in the cellar, but the boy wasn't there. Lucky for him.

When I got home, Steffan, balaclava over his eyes, was up the tree in the back garden.

'Mind you don't fall,' I said automatically.

'Stop fussing. You're worse than our mam for fussing.'

I raised the right eyebrow. 'Yeah, right. Like Mam fusses? Ever?'

I let him into the house, and put the kettle on for a cup of tea while I laid the table for supper. Friday's usually

Chinese takeaway or home-delivery pizza: Mam doesn't do 'proper' cooking, either, so Ceri and I usually do it, even Sunday lunch. Dad's always willing to help, but he's a bit cack-handed, so we encourage him to do Other Things, like giving us extra pocket money.

While I was waiting for the pot to brew, I rang the hospital to see when we could expect Aunty Gwen home. I got through to the ward she'd been on. It wasn't good news. I spoke to the nice sister, who recognised my voice, so she talked to me, and didn't just give me the 'as well as can be expected' guff. She said they'd kept Aunty Gwen in because they weren't happy with her blood pressure.

I thanked her and hung up. Steffan was sitting at the kitchen table, unloading his schoolbag. He had to keep pushing the balaclava up over his eyes to see.

'Got any homework, Hatman?'

He shrugged. 'A bit. I gotta finish reading this book and do a book report on it.'

'Which book's that?'

He looked disgusted. 'I dunno, Ni. Books are *boring*. I hate reading.'

I didn't like to hear him say that. I love reading – always have, since I was tiny, and Dad used to read to me every night at bedtime. 'Reading's fantastic, Steff!' I protested. 'It's like having a key to everything, reading is. There's nothing better than a good book.'

'Yes there is. Computer games. And call me Hatman.'

'But –' I searched for an answer to that one. 'But computer games are just someone else's imagination.'

'Yeah, yeah, yeah. So are books.' He made a sort of

winding motion by his right ear that meant 'hurry up, I'm bored'.

How could I convince him? It dawned on me suddenly that for some reason Dad didn't read to Steffan the way he used to read to Ceri and me. Maybe he didn't have time, because he was always so busy in work these days. 'Look, Steff – sorry – Hatman,' I said, feeling bad that I hadn't even noticed that Steffan had been deprived. 'What if I read to you, every night, before you go to sleep?'

My little brother shrugged. 'Whatever. If you want.'

I didn't just want to – I needed to, for Steffan's sake. If he didn't read, then he wouldn't ever *be* anything . . . Then, the little light went on in my brain.

I was talking to Steffan exactly the same way Mrs Richards art had been talking to me that afternoon. Duh.

CHAPTER NINE

T HE HOSPITAL had open visiting on Saturday, and everyone was going in the afternoon, but because I was off to the match with Rhyming Ryan O'Brien, I'd go in the evening, on my own, instead, which would suit me better. I had to have That Talk with Gwen.

I had butterflies in my stomach all morning. You may think it's daft getting nervous over a date with a bloke, but it was a first date, and I'd fancied him for ages. I tried on every single pair of jeans I owned (four) and every sweater (seven) and still wasn't satisfied. Only one thing for it. Ceri was out with her mates, so I snaffled her best black sweater and a squirt of her expensive perfume, tied up my best Timberland boots, and was waiting by the front door when Ryan's dad pulled up outside the house and honked his horn.

Ryan was sitting in the front seat, so I got into the back and did up my seatbelt. Ryan's dad glanced at me in the mirror and grinned. 'Hiya, Nia. Nice to meet you.'

My ears got hot. 'You too, Mr O'Brien,' I muttered. Ryan said nothing, but turned to give me a grin. It wasn't far from our house to the rugby ground, but by the time we had found a parking space, it was nearly time for kick-off. I wondered if his dad would be sitting with us, but he handed Ryan two tickets and disappeared.

Once he'd gone, Ryan grinned at me again. 'Should

be a great match,' he said. 'The Scarlets are looking good, but we're better.' Inside, he bought me a hot dog, and we munched happily while we found our seats in the stand. Once we were sitting down, Ryan looked around. 'Oh no,' he groaned. 'There's Mouthy Morris up there!'

I turned and looked. It was indeed Morris the Mouth.

'Don't wave at him! He'll see you! It'll be all over the school! I'll never hear the last of it.'

'Last of what?' I didn't understand.

'Well, me. Out with you. Aw, they'll give me hell!'

I scowled. 'What's wrong with being out with me?'

'Nothing! Honest, Nia! Only – well, Dubious Mike knows I – um – like you, but he never told no one. But if Mouthy knows, so will everyone else.'

No kidding, I tell you, for a rugby-playing lad from my school, this was a declaration of undying love! He liked me! And he liked me enough to tell Dubious Mike! My face un-scowled, and a little warm feeling started in the pit of my stomach. 'What did Dubious say?'

Ryan grinned. 'What d'you think?'

'He was Dubious?'

'You got it in one. He said, "Oh, bit dubious, 'bout that, Ry. Why would Nia go for you, Ry? Bit dubious."'

'That,' I said, 'is all *he* knows, right?'

And Ryan O'Brien went bright pink and held my hand!

I glanced back at Mouthy Morris. He gave me a little finger-wave, and clasped his hands in front of his chest. I stuck out my tongue – in a very mature manner, naturally.

It was a great match – we won – so Ryan was happy. We met up with his dad afterwards, and he drove us home. This time, Ryan got in the back with me. His dad turned round. 'I'll get myself a chauffeur's hat, shall I, Ry?'

'Cut it out, Dad!' Ryan muttered.

When we got to my house, Ryan got out of the car and walked up the path with me. 'Thanks for coming, Nia.'

Was he going to kiss me? My stomach churned.

No, he wasn't. Ah well. Mind, his dad *was* sitting outside in the car, I suppose.

'Bye, then. Thanks, Ryan. That was great.'

'Yeah.' He turned to leave. 'See you Monday, then.'

'Yeah.'

'Wanna go to the pictures Sat'day?'

'All right. Yeah. OK. F'ntastic.'

'So long then.'

I watched him get back in the car before I went inside, dreamily taking off my coat and hanging it up. I wandered into the kitchen, where Ceri was making spaggy bol for tea. She did a double take when she saw me.

'That's my sweater!' she snarled. 'I've told you before, Nia. Don't borrow my stuff without asking!'

'Sorry, Ceri. I'd have asked you, honest, but you weren't here, were you?'

'Then you shouldn't have borrowed it. AND you're wearing my perfume! Honest, Nia, there's times when I –'

'But you won't. Because you know you can borrow anything of mine, any time. I won't complain.'

'You haven't got anything I want to borrow!'

Sigh. 'Ah well. Life's a beach, Cer!'

She gave the Bolognese sauce an angry stir. 'Sometimes, Nia, I could strangle you!'

'But you love me really!' I socked her gently on the arm.

'Yeah, right. Anyway, before I forget – Aunty Gwen wants to see you. You'd better go in tonight, after tea.'

'I was going to, anyway. Is she OK?'

Ceri pulled a so-so face. 'Her blood pressure is still very high, the nurse said. They won't let her out until it settles down, so she could be in another week.'

'Poor old Gwenny. They can't seem to make their mind up about her, can they?'

We had our tea, and Dad gave me a lift to the hospital. I'd walk home: it wasn't far, and it wouldn't be completely dark.

Aunty Gwen was sitting up in bed, and she looked thoroughly mutinous. She smiled when she saw me, however. 'Nia! Oh, there's a lovely girl, coming in. Sit down by here and talk to me. Want a grape?'

Her fat lip had gone down, so she wasn't lisping any more. I broke off a small stalk and popped a grape.

'Did you leave the food out like I asked? Did you?'

'Yeah, Aunty. Don't worry. Your – erm – visitor is fed. And I expect he found the clean clothes you'd ironed for him, too.'

'Oh, good –' Then she realised and went still. 'How –'

'I left the key in the back door, and had to go back to the house to get it. I heard a noise and he was down in the cellar. It was, like, really scary, Aunty Gwen, finding some bloke hiding down there.'

'That's all?'

'Not quite. While I was talking to him we heard a noise. It was those boys who mugged you. Your wallet was in your

70

bag, and it's got your address in it, right? And your front-door keys as well. But then –'

Aunty Gwen covered her eyes with her hands. 'Oh, no!'

'Your lodger was about as much good as a Kleenex umbrella. If it hadn't been for this big dog turning up, I don't even want to think what might have happened to me. He scared them off good and proper, I can tell you. I don't think they'll be back – and anyway, they forgot to take the key with them, so they can't get back in.'

Aunty Gwen spread her fingers and peeked out. 'Dog?'

'Yeah. Huge thing it was. Do you know whose it is?'

She gave me a peculiar sort of look. 'Mmm. Sort of.'

'Hell of a dog, Aunty! Size of a house he was, and if it hadn't been for him I'd have really been in the fertiliser. I'm going to buy him a great big bone when you get home, and give it to him.'

'Oh, I don't think that's necessary, dear, not really.'

'Like I said, I wasn't impressed with that bloke, Aunty. Total wimp, if you ask me. Took one look at the muggers and scarpered. Why do you help people like that?'

'Mael is – well, he's a very unusual boy.'

'Huh,' I said, bitterly. 'Personally, I think he's a couple of sausages short of a hot-dog stand, if you know what I mean. Mael, is it? Well, at least he's Welsh. How long has he been bothering you, then, Aunty?'

'Bothering me? He doesn't bother me, Nia! He's helpful and kind, and –' Her voice was rising, and she stopped, grinning weakly at the lady in the next bed, who luckily had her ears stuffed full of hospital-telly earphones.

'Where did you meet him?'

'I didn't *meet* him, Nia. I found him hiding in the garden shed early one morning. He was freezing cold –'

'You could have had a heart attack, finding some strange yob in your shed.'

'I'm not quite that decrepit yet, Nia. Anyway, I got him inside the house, put him by the fire and gave him some hot soup. I gave him a bed for the night, and next day I found some old clothes of your uncle's he could wear. But he got a terrible cold, and I couldn't send him away, could I? So I sort of looked after him until he was better –'

'And now you're stuck with him.'

'Stuck with him? No, dear, not at all! I like having him around. He's lovely company. He makes me feel safe.'

'Safe? But he's useless in a crisis! He's a total wuss!'

'He's a nice boy, Nia. But he's – well, a bit erratic, I suppose.'

'*Erratic?*' I hissed. 'He's a lousy coward and he's scrounging off you. *And* he's not all there!'

'Ssh. Don't be unkind.'

'Sorry, Aunty. But still –'

'He was homeless and needed somewhere to sleep, Nia, so I gave him a home. He's perfectly fine with me.'

'Until he gets in a bad mood and strangles you or something, I suppose!'

'Oh, don't be so dramatic, Nia! He's not going to do that. He's really gentle and sweet.'

'Does he bring you tea in bed and fetch your *Western Mail* every morning, then? Huh. Anyway, where's he live? He must, like, have parents somewhere?'

Aunty Gwen's face went sad. 'His mam died when he was young, so his father brought him up.'

'And? Why doesn't he just go home, then?'

'He wasn't happy. His father didn't understand him. He sounds like quite a horrible man – violent. And that was what did it. Mael – well – everything sort of changed for him, suddenly. He became – um – a different character.'

'Had a breakdown, you mean?' I thought I was sort of understanding what had made Aunty Gwen take in the stray. 'What did his dad do?'

She looked grim. 'He thought he could "cure" Mael.'

'How?' I had a feeling I wasn't going to like her reply.

'By "beating the nonsense out of him". That's what Mael said. Needless to say, it didn't work. He is what he is, and nothing can change that.'

'Poor thing!' I breathed. My mam was off with the fairies, and my dad usually took the line of least resistance – but neither of them ever, ever beat us.

'He had nowhere to go, Nia. So now he lives with me. Since your uncle died, I've been lonely, rattling around in that old place, and he's company. He's no trouble, even when he's . . .' – she glanced at the lady in the next bed – 'you know, reacting badly. Not that he's ever reacted badly to me. And,' she went on, 'since I'm laid up in here, you are going to have to look out for him.'

'Me? Why me?'

'You aren't paying attention, Nia. He's only young. A lonely, frightened boy, the same age as you, no matter how big he is. He needs someone to take care of him.'

'Yes, but –'

'You're going to have to go over to my house every day and make sure he has food and anything else he needs.'

73

Oh, great. Nia Roberts, babysitter to the world's weirdos! I sighed a big sigh. 'If you say so, Aunty. I suppose I can.'

'Oh, good girl. I knew you would. Make sure he has lots of food – he gets very hungry, especially when – I mean, he's a growing boy. Mael likes sausages; you can get him some of those, and he's very fond of liver –'

'That you can forget, Aunty Gwen. I can't even *look* at liver, let alone cook it!'

'Then get some pork or something.'

I held up my hand to stop the flow of instructions. 'Bit of a problem, Aunty Gwen. I get pocket money, but that won't stretch to feeding someone.'

'*Dim problem*! If you go up in my bedroom and open the big wardrobe and take all the shoes out of the bottom, there's a loose plank. You'll find a shoebox underneath.'

I moaned. 'Please don't tell me you keep your life savings in a shoebox in the wardrobe, Aunty Gwen!'

'Why ever not? Why should I pay the bank to look after it? I don't trust banks. They're always out for what they can get, and every time you take your eyes off them they go bust and people lose all their savings. Safer in my wardrobe.'

'If you say so, Aunty. I suppose it's OK – unless there's a fire.'

'I have my electrics checked every autumn, and I've got smoke alarms everywhere, so don't go worrying about that. Take whatever you need for Mael. I should be out of here in a day or two, and then you can forget you ever met him.'

I was looking forward to that . . .

CHAPTER TEN

I STILL had Aunty Gwen's door key with me, so I called at her house on the way home. I called out 'Mael?' as I opened the front door. At least I knew his name now so I could shout at him and he'd know it was him I was swearing at. No answer. I opened the cellar door and did the same. He wasn't there, or if he was, he didn't answer.

It felt all wrong being in Aunty Gwen's house when she wasn't, and even worse creeping up her stairs like a burglar and poking around in her wardrobe. I hauled out about three hundred pairs of shoes, then lifted out the loose floorboard and found the shoebox just where she said it would be. When I took the lid off, I almost fainted dead away. *It was stuffed full of £50 notes!* I'd been expecting a couple of tenners for emergencies – but there must have been hundreds, if not thousands of pounds there! I came over all sweaty at the thought of the muggers! I took one of the bundles and put it in the zipped pocket of my sweatshirt, closed the box and returned it to its hiding place. My hands were shaking. I'd never seen so much money in my life. It was a pretty good hiding place, and it would take a seriously good burglar to find the cash – but all the same, it worried me. Normally I'd have told Dad, and he'd have put the dosh in the bank for her, but I couldn't, could I? He'd probably think I'd been snooping round Aunty Gwen's house while she wasn't there

– and Aunty Gwen didn't want anyone but me to know about Mael. Sigh. Doesn't it get complicated when someone asks you to be economical with the truth? I put all the shoes back, neatly, and got up off my knees.

I let myself out the front door, and went home. Ceri was up in her room, and everyone else was watching a Batman DVD. Hatman/Steffan was sitting so close to the screen that his nose was nearly touching it. 'You'll ruin your eyes, sitting that close,' I said, automatically, but he ignored me. I went and tapped on Ceri's door.

'If you're six feet tall, male, single, rich and gorgeous, come in,' she called. 'If you're not, get lost.'

I went in anyway. 'I'm dark, single and particularly gorgeous, but you can't have everything, Ceri.' I plonked myself on her bed and stretched out.

'Comfortable?' she asked, sarcastically.

'Yes, thanks.' Ceri was sitting at her dressing table sorting her make-up. Tons and tons, most of it hardly used. I like it when she has a sort through – I get her cast-off eyeshadows. I like it better when she prunes her wardrobe, mind! Ceri has a serious clothes habit.

'Ni, what am I going to do?' she asked.

'Give me that sparkly blue eyeshadow?' I said, hopefully.

'No. About Mam and the telly thing.' She tossed me the eyeshadow anyway.

I smeared sparkly azure onto the base of my thumb and watched it glint. I'd hardly given a thought to poor Ceri and her problem with Mam – I'd been far too worried about Aunty Gwen and her lodger. 'Dunno. I s'pose the only thing you *can* do is get on with it. Sort of tough it out.'

'Tough it out how?'

'Well – turn up on Monday for rehearsals and hope she isn't there. If you've got a big part and she's playing a corpse or an extra or something, she probably won't need much rehearsal, will she? And they won't want her the whole time if she's only in one scene. Do you know when she's supposed to be starting?'

Ceri shrugged. 'Nope. She's got to work her notice at the estate agent's, and she's paid monthly, so I suppose she must have at least three more weeks there – I hope!'

'Unless she's got some leave left. You could ask her?'

'Oh, I couldn't, Ni! I'd let something slip! I can hardly look her in the eye as it is. I feel awful about the whole thing. Oh, Ni, do you think I ought to ring Maldwyn Verdun Goldwyn-Jones and tell him I can't do it?'

'I'll smack you if you do! No way, Cer! Are you nuts? This is your big chance – you've got to do it! Unless you want to go on being a fat carrot all your life!'

'Yeah, but –'

'No buts about it. You've got to go for it, Ceri! Look, tell you what, I'll try and find out when Mam's s'posed to start rehearsals, then you'll know how long you've got before – well, you know.'

'That'd help – maybe I could pull a sickie on the day she does her bit?' She sat up, brightening at the thought.

'She's still going to find out when the series comes out, isn't she?'

Ceri slumped again. 'Oh. Yeah. I s'pose. Oh, go on then, find out for me. But don't say anything. Promise?'

I couldn't resist it. 'Mum's the word!' I deftly caught the

flying lipstick, pocketed it and trotted downstairs. I slithered into the sitting room. Two pairs of eyes goggling at Michael Keaton's plastic chest. Dad was reading his library book. I sat down next to Mam.

'Mam?'

'Hmm?'

'You know this acting thing you're doing?' I had her attention instantly.

'Oh, yah?' She went all plum-in-the-mouth when she was talking about her 'career'.

'When are you going to start?'

'About three weeks' time – I told Maldwyn – he's my agent – I can't start sooner because I've got to work my notice. Why?'

Good question! I thought quickly. 'Well, I wondered – I know I haven't got any experience, Mam, but it's nearly half-term, so I thought I could, like, you know, tag along with you to the studio and, like, pick up some work as an extra or something?'

My mam guffawed. 'What, you act? Nooo! I don't think any of you lot have inherited my acting gene! Steffan's good at pretending –'

Hatman scowled at her.

'But – no, Nia, you'd just be in the way. I'm sorry, love. It's just not possible. And in any case, who's going to look after Steffan when I'm on set?'

Steffan shot me a look that said, 'What, you, look after me, Hatman the All-Powerful?'

I didn't say anything. In fact, I bit my tongue. Dad glanced up from his book. I couldn't quite read his expression, but I knew he'd been listening. Anything I said would only cause a row, cos now I was feeling indignant. Why should I have to spend my precious half-term babysitting my little brother? I didn't grudge Mam her chance at another bash at acting – but I might want to be off with Ryan, or my mates, or – or babysitting Mael, if Aunty Gwen wasn't home by then. I toddled back upstairs to Ceri.

'You're OK for three weeks or so,' I said.

My sister blew out a huge, relieved breath. 'Oh, f'ntastic. Perhaps by then my part will be finished and I won't have to be there! How long d'you think it takes to film a telly episode?'

I shrugged. 'Haven't got a clue.'

'We've got a read-through on Monday morning, and then we block out the first scene in the afternoon. That's when we sort of run through the moves with the script. Oh, Ni, it's going to be so great! No more temping for the agency while I try to decide what to do with my life!'

'You ever regret not going to uni, Cer?' I asked idly.

She thought about it. 'Sometimes. Trouble was, even though I got all those As, I couldn't decide what I wanted to do with them. I wanted to go to drama school, but I somehow never got up the energy to apply.'

'Really? I didn't know that! Since when did you want to act?'

'I don't know. It just sounded like fun, and arty, and different, and I always loved being in the school plays, with the rehearsals, and the excitement. But when I asked the careers adviser in school, she said, "You know what people say to drama graduates?" I said no, I didn't, and she sort of sniggered and said, "Big Mac and Fries, please". And now,' –

she gave me a cat-that-got-the-cream grin – 'now I'm going to show that old bat, aren't I?'

'Too true. But – there's still the Mam problem.'

'I know. She's going to throw a technicolour wobbly when she finds out!'

'Why don't you tell Dad what's going on, Cer?'

'You know what he's like. He's hopeless at keeping secrets, especially from Mam, and all hell will break loose if he tells her. The longer she doesn't know, the better. Oh, why is it always me that has the terrible secrets?'

'What, you've had others?'

'Well no . . . Well, 'cept when I was going out with Jason Williams.'

'You went out with *him?*'

She grinned. 'Yeah. For about a month.'

Jason Williams was the local bad boy – everybody knew him. He was always the one pulled in for questioning by the police if anything got vandalised or pinched, or there was a punch-up outside the club or the chippy on a Saturday night. He was a Bad Lot, but oooh! he was a handsome Bad Lot! 'What was it like, going out with him?'

She grinned and wound a strand of hair round her finger. 'Honestly?'

'Yeah.'

'Terrifying! I never knew what he was going to do next, and Dad would have filleted me if he'd found out!'

'So – who dumped who?'

My sister pouted. 'That's for me to know and you to wonder about!'

'He dumped you, then.'

She threw a tube of mascara at me. I was doing well tonight! Eyeshadow, lipstick, and now mascara, too.

'And I suppose you never have any dark secrets from Mam and Dad, right, Miss Goody-Knickers?'

In bed, later, I thought about the sticky-beaks in our village – sneeze in Stryd Fawr and everybody in Lower Merthyr Row gets flu. I wondered how on earth Aunty Gwen had managed to keep Mael secret! I mean, a teenage boy, moving in with an elderly lady? Yet somehow, no one seemed to have noticed, because not one word had leaked. I knew, if it had, someone would have casually let it slip to Mam or Dad. I hoped it would stay that way.

I dropped off to sleep thinking about Ryan O'Brien. I fell asleep with a smile on my face. A big smile.

CHAPTER ELEVEN

Ceri, her new job dangling over her head like Damocles' sword, was totally stressed out by the time she started. (*Who's Damocles?* I hear you ask. Go look it up – that's how I found out.) She was twitching, snapping, slamming doors and flouncing until Dad got fed up with it, and told her to go to her room if she couldn't be pleasant. Steffan was at Cei's house for tea, and Mam tootled off to the hospital to bend Gwenny's ear with tales of the revival of her career.

Dad waited until she got the car safely up the drive without reversing into anything. Then he put down his paper, lowered his glasses and gave me his Number-one Dad stare. 'Right,' he began, ominously. I readied myself for an interrogation.

'Er – cup of tea, Dad?' I asked, getting up.

'No thanks. Sit down, please, Nia. I want to talk to you.'

Scary stuff. 'Oh? What, Dad?' What indeed. Not tidying my bedroom? Being unkind to Steffan? Harbouring secrets from my parents?

'Well, now.' Dad leaned back in his chair. 'About your mother.'

'What about her?'

'I know you don't think she can act – and neither does anyone else – but will you just try to be a little bit understanding? Please? For me?'

'I'm trying, Dad. But –'

'I know you are, *cariad*. Her getting this part means that, with both me and your sister out at work all day, you'll be stuck here looking after Steffan. I know he can be a pain in the bum, but little boys do turn into human beings eventually, and the day will come when you'll really value each other –'

Somehow I doubted that! 'It's not fair, Dad! He doesn't do anything I tell him, and he keeps disappearing and I don't know where he is or what he's up to, and if anything goes wrong I get the blame. That's, like, so unfair! There's stuff I want to do with Mab and –'

'And Ryan O'Brien? No, it's not fair. I grant you that. But I've been thinking.'

'And,' I wailed, 'it means everywhere I go Steffan tags along, and he makes fun of me and my friends! He's a pain and, if I can't find him, I can't go anywhere until I do. He's like a living ball-and-chain. Except he escapes and I can't.'

'I know all that. But your mam needs this chance, Nia. I have hopes of this new thing she's involved in.'

'What?' I couldn't believe my ears. 'You think she's going to turn into a superstar or something?'

'Not a hope. She can't act, *cariad*; I know that as well as anybody. But maybe this time, when she finds out she's going to be playing another extra, or another body in an alleyway, or another unconscious person on a stretcher, she'll take the hint and maybe call it a day.'

'You really think so, Dad?'

He scratched his bald spot and sighed. 'No. Not really. She's always going to want to do it. It's part of what she is.'

'But why, Dad? Why's she like that?'

'Long story, love. Comes down to your nana, really.'

'Nana?' Now, my nana was a character – in the worst possible way. Other people have cuddly grannies that spoil them and let them make a mess of their kitchens. My nana was about as cuddly as a roll of barbed wire, and about as generous. She didn't like kids, even though my mam was the youngest of seven. 'What, *Nana* made her stage-struck?'

'No. Quite the opposite, in fact. Your nana had lost interest in kids by the time your mam came along. If Mam had been a boy, it might have been a different story. But your nana almost totally ignored her, especially after your grancher died. Gwenny more or less brought her up. I think your mam had a sort of secret dream life, that one day she would be rich and famous so everyone in the world would love her – and your nana would be proud of her.'

I was speechless. You somehow don't think of your mam having feelings like that, do you? 'But *we* love her, Dad! I know you do, and me, and Ceri and Steff – we all love her. Why should Nana still matter so much? She's dead, after all.'

'Well – to your mam, Nana's opinion still matters – she spent most of her life trying to please her and make her proud – but it was never going to happen.' Dad shook his head sadly. 'I just thought, if I had a little chat with you, tried to make you understand that just because a person isn't good at something, it doesn't stop them wanting to do it. I mean, I always hoped I'd play for Wales – but I knew I wasn't good enough. She doesn't. Understand?'

I hadn't, before, not properly. But I did now. 'I think so, Dad.' Now would probably have been the time to tell him about Ceri – but I couldn't, could I? I'd promised. And Ceri was right. Dad would only let the secret out, because he could never keep anything from Mam.

'But I'll still be looking after Steffan over half-term, won't I?' I moaned.

Dad smiled. 'Indeed you will. So what if we put it on a professional basis?'

'Professional how?'

'Professional like three quid an hour?'

Would I! Three squids an hour would be, like, awesome! For a, say, seven-hour day that would be – quick jog through the three-times table – twenty-one quid a day! More than a hundred smackers in a week! 'Honest? Can you afford it, Dad?'

'Just about. You deserve some compensation for having your holiday ruined. I'd like you to save some of it, mind. You're going to need money for when you –' He stopped, and I knew exactly what he'd been about to say.

I grinned. 'Don't worry, Dad. I'll save some for uni, I promise.'

Dad grinned back. 'So. Not a word to your mam, and don't tell Steffan, either. Just think, whenever he winds you up, *three quid an hour!* You'll find it makes it a lot more bearable!'

'Oh, it will. Look, Dad, I – I sort of promised Aunty Gwen I'd keep an eye on her house for her. She's a bit worried because the muggers got her house keys and stuff. I'm going to pop over there now, all right?'

He frowned. 'You want me to come with you? I could run you up the road –'

'No you can't. Mam's got the car,' I reminded him. *Thank goodness!* I thought.

'Oh, yes . . . All the same, will you be all right?'

'Yeah. Course I will. No one's going to break into Aunty's house! That would be really stupid. Anyway, Steff's out, and so's Ceri, and you know what she's like for forgetting her door key.'

'I suppose so. Look, take your mobile with you, just in case. Is it charged up?'

'Yes, but I've got hardly any credit.'

'Take mine, then. It's in the kitchen.'

I grabbed the phone from the kitchen table and cradled it in my palm. *Oh, you little beauty! How I want one of you!* I thought. Mine was a bottom-of-the-range, basic, pre-pay thing, but his was a really up-to-date job that did everything except make coffee and tap-dance. But I wasn't going to get one, except when I borrowed Dad's. Then I thought, *three quid an hour, one hundred a week . . .* I could afford to buy one if this acting thing went on long enough! Except I knew I probably wouldn't. I'd stick to my old one. I'd put loads of talk-time on it, though! I pocketed the phone and went out the back door.

The sun was out, although it looked a bit watery. Heavy clouds were coming over from the west, which meant rain before long. Ah well, I'd be back before then. I went the long way round and stopped in at the Spar in Stryd Fawr. I didn't want to go to Mrs Cadwallader's place. She'd start asking and talking if I went into her shop every day and bought loads of food – especially with a £50 note! The supermarket was nice and neutral. I could be anonymous there. I got some frozen chips and a couple of big steaks from the chiller. He probably wouldn't be there, but I'd promised Aunty Gwen

I'd look after her guest even if he was a rotten lousy coward who left girls to get attacked by violent criminals.

I half expected to find the house empty and Mael gone, but he was sitting at the dining table, his head in his hands. He looked up, and I saw his face. He looked, like, totally *down*. 'What's the matter? You look awful.'

He wiped his nose on his T-shirt sleeve. 'Nothing.'

'Yes, there is. You're upset. What's happened?'

'Happened? Absolutely nothing. What could happen? I'm stuck here all day, with no one to talk to. I'm –'

'You're *lonely*?'

He nodded.

'You go out, though, don't you? I was here last night and you were out somewhere.'

'Sometimes I just – have to. I don't speak to anyone, though. I can't.'

I wanted to poke myself in the eye for being so stupid. He wasn't a stray cat that could fend for itself. He might be a rotten coward but he was also a human being. Of course he got lonely. He was about my age, maybe a bit older. He must be bored out of his head stuck in Aunty Gwen's house.

'God, I'm so stupid! Shall I get you some books out of the library? I could lend you some, but you probably wouldn't like mine: they're all a bit girlie. Unless you like fantasy, that is.'

The way his eyebrow went up made me smile. 'Fantasy?' he said. 'You mean, like witches and wizards and –'

'– yeah, zombies and werewolves and crazy stuff like that,' I said, laughing. He laughed too, which made me feel better. 'So, shall I?'

'No point,' he mumbled, looking down at his clasped hands.

'Why?'

'Can't read.'

'You *what?*' I couldn't believe my ears. 'You're how old, fifteen?'

'Yeah.'

'And you can't *read?*'

He shook his head. 'Not very well. I was never in school long enough. When my mam got ill, my dad had to go to work and I stayed home and looked after Mam and the house and stuff.'

'But the truancy people, didn't they come round to find out where you were, why you weren't in school?'

'Once or twice. Then Mam died and me and Dad moved house, so they couldn't find us, because he never bothered to register me with another school. After that, I – well, I left home. I never bothered to go back to school. No point, really, me being the way I am.'

'But – that's terrible! As for the way you are, that could change – I'll help you!' Some of my negative feelings about him had evaporated. Imagine not being able to read! I couldn't imagine anything worse than not being able to curl up with a book.

He shrugged. 'You can't help me.'

'But you *need* to get an education.'

'Why?'

'Everybody needs to learn how to read and write, so you can get a job and stuff.' (I'd only just had this conversation with Steffan!) Another thought struck me. 'And Aunty Gwen isn't getting any younger. She isn't going to live forever. What will you do when she's gone?'

His face went still. He obviously hadn't thought of that. 'I don't know.'

'You've got to start going to school again. You've got to.'

'How? I'd need records from my last school and stuff – wouldn't I?'

He was right. I racked my brains and chewed a bit of hair. Then, 'Got it! You've been living abroad. And you're waiting for your school records to come from – somewhere where there's a war going on or an earthquake or something. Everyone knows that communications go haywire then, and maybe your school got burned down and so your records have got destroyed – it would work, Mael. I promise you it would work.'

'But I can't read!'

'No problem. We'll say you're dyslexic or something. I'll help you, you'll get help in school, and when Aunty Gwen comes out of hospital, she'll help you, too.'

'I – I can't!' Pause. Hope filled his eyes. 'Can I?'

'Yes, you can! You can come to school with me! I'll introduce you as, as, as – my long-lost cousin from Outer Mongolia or something! It would work! Give it a try?'

He stared at me for a long time, his face expressionless. Then, 'Do goldfish climb trees?'

I started to laugh. I was going to have to work on his metaphors, too!

CHAPTER TWELVE

Ceri went off first thing Monday morning to catch the early train to Cardiff. The more I thought about the Mam+Ceri+telly problem, the more it added up to disaster. She and Mam were going to be catching the same train when Mam started, too, every single day. Ceri might manage to hide in a separate carriage one day, but I doubted she could keep it up for long. If TV extras just arrived, lay down, looked dead/injured, got paid and went home, Ceri might get away with it. But extras (extras like Mam, anyway) hang around the studios, watching in case they're needed for anything else, because they're *all* star wannabees. I had this feeling of impending *doooom*.

I took special care getting ready for school. Luckily I wasn't having a BHD (Bad Hair Day) or a ZON (Zit on Nose) day, either. I put on a bit of eyeshadow and mascara – just enough to take the bare-naked look off my face, but not enough to get me spotted by the Head.

My best friend Mably was waiting for me when I got there, hopping with nosiness about my sort-of-date on Saturday. I just about had time to tell her that I had another date for the pictures next Saturday when a male voice, pitched high to imitate a girl, cut into our cosy chat.

'Eeuw! It's Nia! How ya doin', Nia? I saw you out with

Ryan O'Brien.' Mouthy Morris was standing behind us, his hand on his hip, waggling his fingers at me.

'Oh, get lost,' I muttered. 'Get a life, Mouthy.'

'Not me that goes to rugby matches with Ryan O'Brien, is it?' he sneered.

'Didn't know you were that way inclined, Mouthy. Anyway? So what?' I could feel my fists clenching.

'Ignore him, Nia,' Mably said. 'He can't help being, like, emotionally immature and intellectually substandard, and, like, a total cretin.'

I tell you, sometimes Mably is so good with words! We managed to shut Mouthy Morris up between us, anyway.

I didn't see Ryan until lunchtime, when he was eating chips in the yard with Dubious Mike and some other boys. He gave me a Look and a Grin, but didn't come over or say anything. I didn't mind – we had a date for Saturday, and anyway, I hate it when people start 'going out' and wander round the yard hand in hand or with their arms wrapped round each other. I think it looks, like, really *pathetic*. Like, totally, utterly, *sad*.

I kept thinking about Ceri all day, wondering how she was getting on. If I'm honest, I felt a bit envious, my big sister getting 'discovered' like that. Didn't envy the hoo-hah when Mam found out, mind! Still, it would be worth it if Ceri ended up with a career that didn't involve carrots.

I decided to pop into the hospital on my way home from school to see how Aunty Gwen was doing. Attila the Hen was on the reception desk again, but I managed to sneak past her and up to the ward without anyone stopping me.

It was visiting hours – but I bet Attila at reception wouldn't have let me in because of my school uniform. If, that is, she'd seen me!

The curtains were drawn round Aunty Gwen's bed, and voices were coming from behind the flowery cotton, so I lurked a bit, waiting for them to come out. At last the curtains were drawn back, and Dr Shami and a nurse emerged. The doctor glanced at me. 'Oh, hello, dear! Have you come to see your aunty?'

Well, I wasn't there to polish the floors, was I? I nodded.

'That's good. She'll be pleased to see you.'

'How is she?'

Dr Shami frowned. 'Your aunt is improving,' she said, 'but she isn't well enough to go home yet, whatever she says. Her blood pressure is very high, and there are other small signs that all is not well. Perhaps you can talk to her, make her see sense, because she is threatening to leave hospital against our advice.'

'Can I go in now?'

The doctor nodded. 'But don't stay too long – she mustn't get over-excited.' Dr Shami bustled away and the nurse pulled the curtains back and tucked them behind the bed. Aunty Gwen was sitting up, her arms folded, frowning.

'I'm not stopping in by here!' she called after the doctor. 'Don't think you can make me stay, because you can't! Oh, hello, Nia love,' she said, spotting me. 'Tell them I'm all right to go home, will you?'

'No, Aunty, I won't. You aren't all right yet, so you need to stay here a bit longer. I know it's a pain, but there's no point in rushing off home if you're going to end up back in here again, is it? Better get sorted.'

'But I've got to get home!' she hissed. 'I've got to get back to Mael, haven't I? You don't understand, Nia. He can't be left alone.'

'Yes he can. And he's not alone. I'm going to pop in and see him on my way home, after I leave here.' I thought it might be a good idea not to tell her I was going to take him to school with me. She'd only get panicky and upset if I did. But I knew I could hack it. 'I'll look after him, Aunty. You really don't have to worry.'

'Are you sure?' Aunty Gwen grabbed a lump of hospital sheet and screwed it up. 'Anything he wants, mind! He's, he's . . .' Her eyes filled with tears.

'He's what, Aunty?'

'He's like my own son,' she whispered.

Aunty Gwen had never had children. She'd already more or less brought up several of her younger sisters, including Mam, and that'd probably been enough to put her off the idea of having her own. I patted her hand. 'Don't worry, Aunty. I promise I'll see him every day, and make sure there's plenty for him to eat.'

Aunty Gwen leaned towards me, hanging on to my hand. 'He needs lots of red meat, Nia. Lots and lots, all right? Take whatever money you need. I trust you to spend it wisely. I don't need it anyway: I've got my pension . . .' She suddenly looked anxious. 'But those boys took my card, didn't they? How will I get my pension now?'

'Dad's taking care of that with the pensions people, so don't worry about it. Or the money. I won't spend it on anything unnecessary. But when you get out, Aunty Gwen, please will you put the money in the bank or the post office or something?'

She primmed her mouth. 'It was getting money out of the post office that landed me in here, wasn't it? No, it's perfectly safe where it is, thank you *very* much.'

I sighed. 'Oh, all right. Anyway, promise you'll stay here where you're safe?'

She scowled. 'But I don't want to. The food is horrible, and they wake me up four or five times in the night to take my blood pressure and temperature. Do you know, the night before last this silly little madam of a nurse woke me up to give me a sleeping pill! She said I'd been "written up for it", so I had to take it!'

I giggled at that. 'Tell you what, Aunty. I'll get the others to bring in some food for you when they come, all right?' I thought a change of subject was a good idea. 'Did Mam tell you she's got another "starring role"?'

Aunty Gwen winced. 'Oh, aye. She did. At great length. Move over, Catherine Zeta, your mam's on her way.'

'Yeah, right. She doesn't start for another couple of weeks, so you're probably in the best place – she's fizzing about it and driving us all mad. Anyway, it's getting late, so I'm off to see Mael. No more worrying, Aunty Gwen, and no more threatening to do a bunk out of here. Promise?'

Sigh. 'I promise.'

I let myself in at the back door of Aunty Gwen's house. Mael wasn't upstairs, but I could hear noises in the cellar, so I opened the door and went down. I can't say I wasn't the tiniest bit anxious. The light was yellowy-dim, but it was Mael down there. I breathed a sigh of relief. He looked up as I arrived at the bottom of the stairs.

'Hi.' He was looking a lot cheerier than he had the day before, but I'd got over my guilt trip and there was something I needed to get off my chest before we could get properly friendly.

'Hi. Hiding down here, are you, just in case?'

'In case of what?'

'In case I get attacked again. You scarpered a bit sharpish, didn't you? If it hadn't been for that big dog, anything could have happened to me. It nearly did!'

'But I was –'

'I don't care what you were. You dumped me right in it! I don't mind helping you out for Aunty Gwen's sake, but the least you could have done was back me up.'

'But I – I didn't –'

I stopped him. 'Talk to the hand: the ears ain't listening. If anything like that ever happens again, I'd like to think you'd back me up better than last time, OK?'

He sighed. 'I will, I promise.'

'Fine, then, all forgotten. Air's cleared. What you doing?'

'I can't just sit about moping – there's useful stuff I can do for Gwen while she's away. I mopped the kitchen floor this morning, and now I'm tidying the cellar. There's loads of junk down here. I think it's been here for years. Look what I found in that old trunk!'

He held out a big book, covered in cracked brownish leather. 'Photographs!' I took it and opened it. The photographs were the same old-fashioned prints that hung on the walls upstairs, and – when I looked closely – I saw the same weird person, all muffled up, that featured in the others. 'Look,' I said, pointing. 'Ryan and me spotted this the other day. See this bloke?' Mael looked over my shoulder. 'He's in loads of pictures – at least, I think it's a he. You can't tell: he's so muffled up.' I flicked over the dusty pages. 'There he is again – and look, everyone else is in summery clothes, and he's muffled up as if it's twenty below freezing.'

Mael was silent, and when I looked up at him, he was staring at me oddly.

'What?' I demanded.

'You don't know?'

'Know what?'

'Oh, never mind.'

Riiiight. I so hate that, when somebody says something and then says, 'Oh, never mind.'

'Wha-a-a-at?'

'Oh, I dare say Aunty Gwen will tell you eventually.'

'Tell me what?'

'Oh. It's a heredity thing. That guy felt the cold. Some people feel the cold more than others. It comes down to genes and stuff. I mean, where did you get your blue eyes?'

'From my mam. Don't know where I got my stupid feet from though.'

'Well, there you are. We've all got bits that go back to the year dot.'

'I suppose. I've never really thought about it.'

'Well, I have. Lots.'

'Why?'

'I've got the same thing – it's sort of – um – a hereditary

disease. My dad thought it was a problem I could control if I put my mind to it. He was wrong. I am what I am.'

'Aren't we all?' I agreed. Maybe he was gay . . . Time to change the subject. 'You hungry?' I asked.

CHAPTER THIRTEEN

S TEFFAN had laid the table, and I had the spuds peeled and the chops defrosted by the time Ceri came back from Cardiff, all pink and bubbling, bursting to tell everyone about her day. She couldn't, of course, because of Mam, but she kept pulling excited faces at me all through tea. As soon as we'd finished eating, and Mam and Dad and Steffan were settled down to watch the telly, Ceri and I slipped upstairs to her bedroom. I hurled myself across the bottom of her bed, making the springs twang.

'Tell me quick, Ceri! How'd it go?' I whispered.

She fell back on her pillows. 'Oh, Nia! It was the best fun I've ever had in my whole life. And you know who else is in it? . . . Only Pietro Annigoni Probert, that's all!'

'Oh, wow, Cer! What's he *like*?'

'Gorgeous looking – but really, really nice as well. He was so kind – he helped me loads with the scene when we were rehearsing. He knew I was really nervous, and he didn't get ratty with me at all. He says I can call him Pete! He's so gentle and kind and – oh, he's just lovely!'

I slapped both hands over my eyes. 'Don't tell me – he's gay, right?'

'No way!'

'Good. Does that mean he's Available, then? Well, more

or less available, anyway.' As if someone that famous would be interested in Ceri!

She went scarlet. 'Well – yeah. I s'pose. More or less.' She twisted the signet ring she always wore on her little finger, a sure sign with Ceri that whatever she was going to say next wasn't necessarily totally, absolutely, entirely true. 'Can't say I've really thought about it, actually.'

'Liar, liar, pants on fire!' I sang, and she poked me with her foot and grinned sheepishly.

'Well, all right. It did cross my mind, just for an instant. But there's no way he'd even look at me. I mean, he's really famous, and I'm just – well, me.'

I decided to be, like, really kind, though I didn't believe what I was saying. I mean, Pietro Annigoni Probert? My sister? Not gonna happen, is it? 'Don't see why not. You're not bad-looking in a pink sort of way, and you do pay for dressing – except as a fat carrot!'

She kicked me and pulled a face. 'Less of the fat, you. But seriously, Nia – I'm just me, aren't I? I'm nobody important, not like him. He's been really famous since he was in that Anthony Hopkins film when he was a kid.'

'But then he stopped being a cute kid and grew up.'

'Into an even cuter bloke! He could have anyone he wants. Why would he even look at me?'

'Why wouldn't he?' I argued. Ceri is actually very pretty, and she hardly ever has BHDs or ZONs or HFDs (Horrible Fat Days). No. It's only me that gets them, unfortunately. I probably get her share as well. Life's so unfair sometimes.

'He just wouldn't, all right? Anyway, when Mam starts work, Pietro's going to find out she's my mother, and when all hell breaks loose, which I just know it will, he's hardly going to want to get involved with me, is he? He'll probably be off like a rat up a drainpipe. Even if he's noticed me, which I doubt. Anyway,' – she twisted her ring again – 'I'm not really that interested, actually.'

'Yeah, right. Your nose is growing, Ceri!'

We stayed, rabbiting, in her room until Dad stuck his head around the door and beetled his eyebrows at me, which meant, 'Bed, Nia!' By the time I left, mind, I'd acquired a pot of brown eyeshadow and Ceri's new pink T-shirt that she'd handed over in a burst of sisterly generosity, and I wasn't argufying about *that*.

Tuesday afternoons in school are fairly deadly – double games, two hours of cold misery on the hockey pitch.

Anyway, one-fifteen saw me sidling through the back school gate and off to Aunty Gwen's. I stopped in at the Spar and picked up some goodies for Mael and, lugging plastic bags, let myself in at the garden door. Mael was on his hands and knees, weeding. He stood up, brushing earth off his hands, when he saw me. He relieved me of the carrier bags, and I followed him into the kitchen.

'What, no school this afternoon?' he asked, selecting an apple and taking a healthy chunk out of it. He had strong white teeth, and it crossed my mind again that he was quite good-looking. His hair was dark and a bit shaggy, and what with his curious golden-brown eyes and thick dark lashes. If it weren't for Ryan, I might – well, never mind. There's Ryan, right?

'I sort of bunked off.' I put a packet of sausages in the

fridge, and some salad in the crisper at the bottom. 'It's only games, and I hate games, so –'

'I'd love to play games,' Mael said wistfully. 'Specially rugby.'

'Oh, shoot!' I said, suddenly realising something. 'If you're coming to school on Monday, you're going to need clothes, aren't you? Uniform, games kit and stuff, right?'

'Does that mean I can't go?'

I wasn't sure if he was disappointed or not. 'No. It means we have to go shopping, like right now.'

'But what about money?'

'*Dim problem*. Aunty Gwen's seen to that.'

'You told Gwenny I'm going to school?'

'Weeeell – not exactly. I didn't want to, like, stress her out when she's not well. Don't worry. I'll tell her soon. When she gets home, maybe. Look, have you eaten?'

He shook his head.

'Right. You make yourself a sarnie – there's sliced bread in the bag, look, and ham as well – and I'll go and get some cash. Then we'll go shopping.'

I raided Aunty Gwen's secret bank, tucked £200 away in my purse, and when Mael had eaten, off we went. I kept my eyes open for the Hobby Bobbies, but they must have been off somewhere, fighting crime. We hopped on a bus into town, and went to a couple of department stores before we managed to find cheapish school kit. I got him everything from the skin out, including boxer shorts, shoes, trainers, socks, and rugby kit. He was a bit worried at first, but then he got the bit between his teeth and started to enjoy it. We bought some decent jeans and a couple of tees and sweat-tops, too, so he wouldn't have to go on wearing Aunty Gwen's, like, totally grotty choices. She's great, my aunty, but when it comes to what kids wear, she doesn't have much idea.

By the time we got back to the house, we were having, like, a really good time, laughing and joking and teasing. We went through the garden door and into the back of the house, unloaded all the parcels, and then I looked at my watch and nearly died. It was ten to five, and Steffan would have been waiting for ages to be let in. He so wasn't going to be a happy Hatman.

'Oh, shoot!' I muttered. 'Gotta go or I'm gonna be in so much trouble. Look, see you tomorrow, OK?'

'OK. See you.' Mael was preoccupied, unpacking his school stuff, holding black trousers up against himself, his eyes shining and face rapt.

I got in just before Mam, and Steffan was seriously not happy. 'I've been bloomin' stuck out here for flippin' hours 'n' hours, Nia!' he complained. 'Iss not fair, me not having a key. Why weren't you home from school at the normal time? Why're you so late? Where've you been? I'm telling Mam you were late home. I was dying for a wee. I was nearly busting!'

'Oh, come on, Steff! I said I'm sorry. I got held up, all right? If you're busting, go to the loo and stop going on about it.' Wrong reaction. I should have been a bit grovelling. That would have cheered him up.

'I couldn't wait any longer, so I went in the bushes. I'm still telling Mam. I bet you got detention!'

'No I didn't. I was just –' I searched around for an excuse

that wasn't really a lie. 'Not that it's any of your business, but I was – I was talking to someone, all right?'

'I bet it was that nerd Ryan O'Brien.'

'Mind your own business. And he isn't a nerd.'

Steffan made kissy noises and ran upstairs before I could wallop him. Kid brothers can be such a pain sometimes. What do I mean, sometimes? Like, *always!*

Mam came in then and had a go at me because I hadn't set the table or emptied the dishwasher or done anything at all useful. Ceri had left a message on the answering machine to say she'd be late home and not to wait for her, to go ahead and eat, and then Dad arrived in a foul mood because the car was playing up.

'What's the matter with it?' I got the mats out of the drawer and started laying the table.

'Who knows? The engine's making weird noises, and it seems to be losing power. I've got it booked into the garage tomorrow.'

'But I *need* it tomorrow!' Mam took her head out of the freezer to glare at him. 'Honestly, Bryn, how thoughtless! Just when I need the car most, you go and put it in the garage for repair!'

'Wouldn't be much good to you the way it is, my lovely. Anyway, why do you need it? You're only going to work, aren't you?'

Her face went pink with excitement. 'No! I suddenly realised I had some holiday time left – I've finished at the estate agent's, so I'm going to the studios tomorrow!'

'But I thought – I thought you –' Dad and I said together. 'What?'

'I thought you weren't starting the acting stuff for a couple of weeks yet,' Dad said, v-e-e-ry carefully. 'What do they want you early for?'

Mam pouted at her reflection in the kitchen mirror, lowered her chin and batted her eyelashes at herself. 'Well, I'm not sure they do. But my studio pass came in the post this morning. I can get in there any time, so I thought I'd go early. You never know: they might need someone for something. After all,' she said grandly, 'I'm not just any old extra. I've acted before, haven't I?'

Well, that was arguable.

'Which was why I needed the car, Bryn. Ah well, I'll just have to go on the train, I suppose.'

Dad's eyes met mine. He groaned, very, very quietly, so she wouldn't hear. 'Be afraid. Be *very* afraid. Tomorrow . . . it begins.'

Gulp. He was worried *now*? He didn't know the half of it! Oh, Ceri, where are you?

CHAPTER FOURTEEN

I WAS in bed by the time Ceri came home, and so were Mam and Dad. A car drew up outside, a car door slammed, and then I heard Ceri's key in the lock. I crept out of bed and lurked on the landing until she came upstairs. I didn't put the light on in case I woke anyone, and she shot about a mile in the air with fright.

'Aaagh!' she squeaked. 'Don't *do* that!' She grabbed my arm and dragged me into her bedroom. 'Close the door, quick.'

I shut the door and she put on the bedside lamp. Her face was flushed, her eyes were shining, and a smug grin stretched from ear to ear. 'Guess what?'

'Dunno, but –' I wasn't looking forward to telling her about Mam.

'I've been out to dinner with Pietro! Pete.'

My jaw dropped open. 'You're joking! What, on a date, kind of thing?'

'Uh-huh! Me! On a date with Pietro Annigoni!'

I plonked onto her bed to listen, all thoughts of Mam and the TV studios driven from my brain. 'How cool is that! Tell me! Tell me!'

'All right, but you're not to tell ANYONE, right? It was just one date: it doesn't mean anything, not really.'

I suddenly felt sick. It might not mean anything to Pietro Annigoni Probert, but it obviously meant an awful lot to my big sister. I hoped she wasn't cruising for a bruising, so to speak. I pulled myself together. 'So – where did you go?'

'This fantastic Italian place down the Bay – it was *sooo* wonderful, Nia! – all the waiters recognised him, and he got his "usual table" and "usual wine" and stuff like that. And they called me *senorita*, and *bellissima* and stuff!'

'And he drove you home?'

'Yeah – in his sports car.' She spreadeagled herself on the bed, the big, soppy grin still in place.

'And did he – you know?'

'What, kiss me?' She smiled, dreamily. 'Only my hand – but honest, Ni, I felt my whole body go fizzy!' She giggled suddenly. 'Mind, that might be something to do with all the wine I drank. I feel a bit skew-whiff. Better get to bed – I've got a long day tomorrow – but I probably won't sleep!' She sat up and grabbed my hand suddenly. 'Don't tell anyone, Nia. Swear?'

'Double swear. Not a word. Lips sealed.' I did the closed mouth, zippy thing. And then took a deep breath. 'Look, Cer, there's something you need to know.'

'Is it going to upset me? Because if it is, I don't want to know. Mind, I don't think *anything* could upset me, not tonight!'

Wrong, Ceri. I let her have it straight: better than stringing it out. 'Mam got her studio pass in this morning's post; she had some holidays left and so she quit her job early. She's going to the studio tomorrow.'

You ever pop somebody's bright, shiny bubble and watch them collapse? Not nice, is it? Ceri went still, her face changed, and she sagged. 'Oh, *no!*' She sank back onto the bed, her arm across her eyes.

'*And*,' I went on, feeling as if I were kicking a puppy, 'the car's on the blink, so Dad's putting it in the garage for repair and so Mam'll be going in by train.'

'Oh, *noooo!*' she said again. 'What am I going to do, Nia? She'll spoil everything.'

I chewed my fingernails. 'I don't know. I've been worrying about it all evening, and I can't think of anything, short of kidnapping her and locking her up until you've finished recording, but Dad might notice if she went missing.'

'There must be something! *Think!*'

'The only thing I can think of is to somehow try to delay her leaving the house. No, that wouldn't work. She's got the acting bit between her teeth. Nothing short of a nuclear holocaust would stop her, and I'm not sure that would.' Then I had a thought. 'Ceri, what time's the first train in the morning?'

'No idea.' She sat up, slowly. 'But I see what you're getting at. If I catch the earliest, earliest train, maybe we won't be on the same one. That'll give me a bit of a head start. She surely won't make a scene at the studios – will she?'

Personally, I wouldn't have placed a bet on it. What, Mam the Drama Queen not making a scene? Yeah, right.

'That's what I'll do, then. If I can get out first, I can get to the studios before her. The director seems quite nice – perhaps if I tell him she's my mam before she arrives, it won't come as a shock –'

And then what? I thought. *Introductions all round and Mam will sit back and watch Ceri be a star? That's so not going to happen!* Ah well. Nothing I could do.

But it turned out there was . . .

Mam was so keen to get to the studio that she was up long before dawn, all ready to go. Ceri looked totally panic-stricken when she came downstairs and found Mam already dressed, full slap on, taking strands of hair out of their pink plastic rollers in front of the mirror.

'Erm – bit early, Mam?' she stammered.

'You never know, Ceri. There might be another little part I could do,' she twittered, chucking rollers on the sideboard. 'Maybe a crowd scene or something.'

Yeah, right. Ceri was sending frantic eyebrow messages behind Mam's back. She was ready to go – but then, so was Mam. What could I do? Spur of the moment – I gasped, whimpered, and fell in a neat heap on the carpet, groaning loudly and clutching my stomach. Mam stared. Steffan reached for the milk for his frosty-pops, totally unconcerned, and Ceri slipped out the front door, throwing me a grateful look.

'What on earth's the matter, Nia?' Mam said.

'Grooooooan.'

She bent over me. 'Are you ill? What's the matter? Get up! I've got a train to catch! Oh, please don't be ill! If I'm not there early someone else might get my part!' She flung open the door and hollered up the stairs. 'Bryn? Come down now! Nia needs you!' She bent over me again.

I moaned, pathetically, and raised a weak hand to my face. 'Ohhhh!' I murmured in my best dying-of-the-plague-

or-worse mode. 'Ooooohhhh! My stomach hurts! I feel so ill –'

'Oh, for heaven's sake!' she snapped. 'Bryn!' she yelled again. 'Get down here now! Look, Nia, you'll be OK. I've got to go. I'll miss the train.'

I reached out a groping hand to detain her. Fat chance. The front door slammed behind her and I heard her high heels rapping down the drive. I sat up and put my head in my hands.

Steffan dropped his spoon into his cereal bowl and looked at me sceptically. 'Nia, you can't act for toffee. You're worse than Mam!'

Dad bumbled into the room, his face worried, and saw me sitting on the floor, my head in my hands. 'Nia? What's the matter, sweetheart?'

Well, he had to know sooner or later – and if Mam and Ceri were going to be in the same studio today – maybe even on the same train – it was time Dad was told what was going on. 'Um, Dad? There's something I've got to tell you.'

Steffan was agog by now, his eyes wide, his mouth open. 'Steffan,' I snapped, 'go to school.'

'Can't. Iss too early. Anyway, I want to know what's going on.'

'Well, you can't. Go and call for Cei.'

'Aww! Iss not fair! Nobody ever tells me anything!'

'Tough,' I snapped. 'I need to talk to Dad.'

Mutinously Steffan got his school stuff and stropped out the front door.

'Right, how about a cup of tea, Dad?' Me, delaying the inevitable.

'*No!*' he said. 'My teeth are gritted, Nia, see?' He bared his teeth at me. They were. 'Tell me what's going on or I swear I'll throttle you!'

'Oh, that's nice from my father, isn't it?'

'Get on with it, will you?'

'Ah. OK. It's like this . . .' And in a few well-chosen words, I told him.

He sat down with a thump. 'You mean –' he said, weakly, 'your mam – and Ceri – same studio . . .?'

'. . . and Ceri's got a starring role, yes,' I finished for him. 'Second lead.'

'Well, it could be worse,' he said slowly, 'but I'm blowed if I can see how.'

'Ceri's hoping they won't let Mam on set – she's only an extra, after all, and they won't want a load of people hanging around getting in the way, will they? From what Mam's said in the past, the extras hang around in the Green Room –'

'– the canteen, actually.'

'– only Mam likes to call it the Green Room – and wait until they're sent for. So with any luck, Ceri might be able to stay out of her way. Maybe they'll send the extras home if they aren't needed.'

'Let's hope. But sooner or later, your mam will find out, and then – oh, Lordy Lordy Lordy!' he groaned.

'I'd rather not be here either,' I agreed with his unspoken end-of-sentence.

'Still.' He grinned, suddenly. 'Good for Ceri, eh? Look, you're going to be late for school if you don't get a wiggle on.'

Well, fiddle-de-dee, so I am! I thought. *Maybe I won't go.*

But then the little angel that sits on the opposite shoulder to the little devil who also whispers in my ear, pointed out that my exams were so close they were treading on my heels, and it was time I did some work. And you know what? I listened. I went to school, in full uniform, no make-up, and Put My Nose To The Grindstone. Poor Mrs Yates, my maths teacher, looked almost pathetically grateful to see me in her class. Well, she was going to have to get used to it. My conscience had kicked in, and I knew I had to do some work.

On the way home from school I popped into Aunty Gwen's house, but Mael was fast asleep on the couch, snoring. I didn't disturb him, just left a couple of cans of beans and sausages on the kitchen table. He could warm those up and make some toast if he was hungry.

Steffan was waiting on the back doorstep when I chugged up the path. 'Oh, you're home early, that's good,' he said. 'It's always nice when you're home early. You *are* my big sister, after all.'

I stopped, the key poised in front of the lock. 'You what?'

'I said –'

'I know what you said. But who are you? What have you done with my little brother? Are you an alien from Planet Boodlephlox? Shall I take you to my leader?'

'Oh, har har, very funny. I'm just being nice.'

'I know. That's what's worrying me. What do you want? And where's your balaclava, Hatman?'

'Oh, I'm not Hatman any more. I'm Technoman now.'

I didn't ask what Technoman got up to. He'd certainly have superpowers, and I definitely didn't want them used on me. 'Oh. OK. Lay the table, please, Technoman. I've got stacks of homework.'

'All right. But only if you'll tell me what you and Dad were talking about this morning.'

I prodded the end of his nose, gently. 'Sticky-beak. You're so clever, Technoman, use your Special Powers to find out, yeah?'

He scowled, blew a raspberry at me and hurtled upstairs, making electronic noises. I sighed. Lay the table myself, then. I'd picked up the morning's *Western Mail* from the mat, and chucked it on the sideboard for when Dad came in.

Mam arrived at around four-thirty, full of the joys of spring, which meant (hooray!) that Ceri had managed to keep out of her way – at least for today.

'Hi, Mam, how'd it go?' I asked.

'Oh, it was fantastic! There were loads of people there I knew, and I've been catching up on all the gossip. The day's gone by in a flash.'

'Did you get any work today?'

'No. The director was lovely, and thanked me for turning up, but he hasn't got anything for me until later.' She shrugged. 'No problem. Do you know, though, I'm absolutely shattered. Must be the excitement and the early start this morning. Will you sort out dinner, Nia? I'm going to have a bit of a lie-down.'

She disappeared upstairs and I sighed and investigated the fridge. Still the rhubarb yoghurt (which everybody hates) a dried-up bit of cheese, three eggs and a cold sausage. Nothing to inspire any Mastercheffery. Nothing else for it. Off to Mrs Cadwallader's for supplies. It was time I showed my face there. I took some money from the tea caddy and trotted down the road.

The sign on the door said 'CLOSED', but it was far too early for Mrs Cadwallader to shut up shop, so I tried the door and it opened. She must have flipped the sign by mistake, or someone was trying to be funny. Mrs Cadwallader wasn't in the shop, but the door to the back room was ajar, so she probably wasn't far away. I got some bacon out of the chiller, tomatoes and mushrooms, and some sausages – that would be quick and easy, and it was something everyone liked – slapped my purchases on the counter and leaned over to see where Mrs Cadwallader was. I hung around for a bit, but she didn't appear. I opened and shut the shop door so that the bell dinged a couple of times, but she still didn't come. Ah well. I found a paper bag and a pencil and left her a note of what I'd taken, added up the cost and promised I'd stop in next day to pay. I took a carrier bag from behind the counter and stuffed my groceries in it, and was about to head off home when I heard a noise from the back room. It sounded like a groan.

CHAPTER FIFTEEN

I COCKED my head and listened: there it was again. It *was* someone moaning! I went round the other side of the counter and listened. This time I heard a weak voice calling, 'Help me! Is anybody there? Hello? Help!'

I pushed open the door at the back of the shop and cautiously went through into a short dark corridor that led to a storeroom full of boxes of crisps and stuff, and a second, closed door at the end. The light filtering through from the shop was fairly dim, but I couldn't see anyone in the storeroom. I opened the door at the end of the corridor and stuck my head into Mrs Cadwallader's sitting room. 'Mrs C?' I called. 'You all right?'

'Who's that? Oh, please help me!'

She was laying on the floor behind the sofa. Her crumpled face was dead-white, streaked with blood trickling from a gash in her scalp. 'Oh, Nia, oh, oh, Nia. I'm so glad to see you, dear! I'm in such a state.'

I knelt beside her. 'Oh, Mrs Cadwallader! What happened? Did you have a fall?'

'No . . . Two boys, two horrible boys. They came into my shop and, and they, they . . .' Tears poured down her face, mingling with the blood. 'They pushed me in here, Nia, and when I tried to stop them, they hit me! I think they took my money!'

'Don't cry, Mrs C. You're safe now. I'll phone for an ambulance. Stay there, all right?' I don't know where I thought she might go, so it was a pretty dumb thing to say, but hey, it was a crisis, right? I went back into the shop, dialled 999 on the wall phone, and asked for an ambulance. I'd always wanted to dial 999, since I was a little kid, but right now I was wishing I didn't have to. It wasn't until after I'd hung up that I thought about fingerprints, but then, I imagine robbers probably don't hang about their crime scenes making phone calls, do they?

Fair dos, the ambulance people were there in a matter of minutes, although it seemed like hours I spent holding Mrs C's hand. The paramedics immediately got to work on her, giving her oxygen, putting a sterile dressing on her head wound and supporting her neck with a spinal board, before loading her onto a stretcher.

One of the paramedics patted my back. 'You did well, love. You'll be all right now? You're not hurt, are you?'

'No, I'm fine – just came in for some stuff and I heard her call out.'

'Did you ring the police as well as us?'

I hadn't. I'd been too worried about Mrs Cadwallader dying on me. 'I'll call in the station on my way home.'

'No, don't bother, love – we'll do it. They'll understand. But she's had a bad shock and she's pretty weak, so perhaps it's just as well they aren't fussing round her right now. Once she's settled, they can go to the hospital to interview her.' He glanced around the shop. 'I wonder what they took.'

'Money, she said. Also,' I pointed behind him, 'there used to be cigarettes in that glass case, and it looks as if they've

115

taken all the chocolate, too – those trays on the counter are usually full of Mars bars and stuff –'

The paramedic sniffed. 'Someone with the munchies, I shouldn't wonder. Hmm.'

'On drugs, you mean?' I said. 'My aunty got mugged the other day – that was two boys, as well. Maybe it was the same ones. D'you think they've left fingerprints? You'd better tell the police they'll need to send a SOCO team.'

The paramedic raised an eyebrow and grinned. 'SOCO, is it?'

'Scene of Crime Officers,' I informed him.

'Yeah. I know. Anyone ever tell you that you –'

'I know, I know. I watch too much telly.'

'That'd be it.' He patted me again. 'You did well, for a telly addict. Good lass.' Then he climbed into the back of the ambulance and they clamoured off towards the hospital, lights flashing.

The shop was in the middle of a row of terraced houses – it had once been a house itself, and the house next door had one of those overgrown hedges that are always messy with bits of sweet wrappers and newspaper caught up in them. Dangling from one of the overhanging twigs was a black baseball cap. Not Mrs Cadwallader's style at all. Little-light-goes-on-over-head. I reached up and unhooked it. Maybe it belonged to one of the robbers. I'd drop it off at the police station after school the next day. The police would probably want a statement from me, anyway. I shoved the hat into my pocket and trotted off, bursting with the news.

Everyone was home and starving by the time I got back. Ceri gave me an eyebrow wiggle and a grin, which told me that everything had gone OK that day. '*Talk later!*' she mouthed at me, and I nodded. I spread the news about Mrs Cadwallader while I grilled sausages and bacon and fried tomatoes and stuff. 'I'll bet it was the same two that attacked Aunty Gwen,' I finished, slapping full plates onto the table. 'They must be targeting old ladies.'

'What sort of a boy does that?' Dad said disgustedly. 'Haven't they got mothers and grannies? What's the matter with them?'

'BRRREEET!' Technoman bleeped. 'I WILL GO AFTER THEM. TECH-NO-MAN WILL NOT NEVER SLEEP UNTIL ALL CRIM-IN-ALS ARE DE-FEA-TED AND IN-CAR-STIF-FER-ATED.'

'That'd be "incarcerated",' I corrected him.

'BREEEET! TECH-NO-MAN IS AL-WAYS RIGHT. TECH-NO-MAN WILL FIGHT CRIME IN THE STREETS AND IN THE PARKS AND IN THE SKIES A-BOVE OUR TOWN.'

'Is that so?' Dad grunted. 'Well, as long as Technoman does his homework first, and is in bed by eight . . .'

Steffan gave him a disgusted look. 'TECH-NO-MAN HAS NO BEDTIME,' he intoned.

'Technoman is asking for trouble,' Dad remarked. 'AN-Y MIN-UTE NOW.'

'Aren't you interested in my day, Bryn?' Mam asked, nibbling at a piece of bread and butter. It didn't matter whether he was interested or not, because she told us all anyway, until our eyes glazed over with boredom. When we'd finished our tea – which was more like supper by the time we got round to it – Steffan and Ceri stacked the dishwasher. Dad followed me into the living room and shut the door behind him, but didn't switch on the telly.

'Looks like Ceri got away with it!' he whispered.

'Yeah, today –' I whispered back. 'Look, Dad – don't let on to Ceri that I told you, all right? I promised her I wouldn't. She'll be mad if she finds out.'

He looked hurt. 'Why? Can't I be trusted?'

'Well, yes. Mostly. Only, you – well, you aren't very good at keeping secrets from Mam, are you?'

He grinned. 'Not usually. But no worries with this one, *cariad*! Self-preservation has definitely kicked in. Mind you, I'm not entirely in favour of my kids keeping secrets from their parents – but –'

Mam came in then, and zapped on the telly. I got fed up after about five minutes of not being able to hear the programme for: *Will you look at how wooden she is! . . . Look, she's supposed to be dead and you can see her breathing* . . . and wandered into the kitchen where Ceri was wiping down surfaces and tidying up. Steffan had disappeared 'to do his homework' but there were suspicious bleeps coming from his bedroom.

'How'd it go?' I whispered.

'Come upstairs and I'll tell you,' she whispered back.

When we were safely in her room, she shut the door, drew the curtains and we settled on her bed, her at the top leaning against the headboard, me at the bottom, propped against the footboard.

'It's been the most fantastic, wonderful day!' she

breathed. 'I ran through my first scene with Pietro without a script and it went really well. When we'd finished, he said I was a rising star, took my hand in front of everybody and kissed it! How cool is that?'

I felt a bit jealous. I wouldn't mind being a star – except I didn't want to do the acting bit that went with it. I only had to *look* at a stage and I forgot my name, let alone anything else. 'Phantasmagorical! And you managed to keep out of Mam's way, too?'

'Yeah. I managed to catch the early train, and Mam was running into the station just as it pulled out, so she missed it, which was a relief. Thanks for the diversion.'

'No problemo. And you managed to avoid her all day?'

'Yeah. When I got to the studios, I wondered if I ought to tell someone, but decided to keep quiet. At least until the filming starts. I think Mam's bit is right at the end, so unless they shoot the scenes out of order, I should be OK for a while. If I only knew what scene they want her for, I could relax a bit, but –'

'And what about the Hunk to end all Hunks?'

She went pink. 'What, Pietro?'

'There's another Hunk I don't know about? You seeing him again?'

She rolled over on the bed and hugged herself. 'Yeah. We're going to a party on Saturday night, in that big hotel down the Bay, the one with the funny roof that Captain Jack keeps standing on in *Torchwood*. I can't wait!'

I started to say, 'Just don't –' I was going to say, 'Don't get too serious – don't get hurt.' But I didn't. After all, what's the use? If you really fancy someone, you don't stop and think about stuff like that, do you? It wouldn't have made any difference, whatever I said. So I changed it in mid-sentence. 'Just don't forget any of it. You have to come back and tell me all about it.' Maybe it was me being a bit jealous, though I didn't mean to be, but at the back of my mind was the thought, *What does Pietro Annigoni Probert want with someone like Ceri when he could have anybody?* I mean, she's my sister and I love her but hey, she's not, like, *that* special.

'I will, I promise. Well –' she grinned. 'Some of it, anyway!'

I sat up suddenly. I heard a noise at the bedroom door. I put my finger to my lips, crept across the floor and flung it open. Technoman fell backwards on his bum. I grabbed the front of his T-shirt, hauled him to his feet and dragged him inside. 'He was listening, Ceri! You revolting little microbe, Steffan!'

He disengaged my fingers disdainfully. 'I wasn't listening. I just – um – bent down to do my laces.'

I looked pointedly at his Velcro-fastened trainers. 'Yeah, right.'

He didn't even blush. 'So I was listening. So what? I didn't hear much. Only that she's got a date with someone on Saturday. Who cares? He's probably a real geek and a nerd and a fatplong anyway.'

'A fatplong?' That was a new one on me.

'Yeah. A fatplong. You don't know what that is?'

'Bet you just made it up.'

He sniffed. 'Didn't.'

'Did.'

'Did not.'

'Oh, cut it out, you two!' Ceri said, exasperatedly. 'Go away, Steffan. It must be your bedtime anyway.'

'It is, nearly. Only –'

'What?'

'Nia promised she'd read to me. Before I go to sleep. Didn't you?' He looked at me appealingly.

'Oh, all right. Go and get into your pyjamas and give me a shout when you've brushed your teeth. What'll I read to you?'

He shrugged. 'Dunno. You choose. Nothing mushy, mind. I can't stand mushy stuff.'

I chose a book I'd loved when I was little, about this kid who was apprenticed to Merlin and couldn't keep out of trouble. I sat on the end of Steffan's bed and read the first chapter, after which he begged for another. This was good. Little Mr *I Don't Like Books* was enjoying a story! 'If I read another chapter, that's the last, right?'

He nodded. I got halfway through the first page and he was asleep.

CHAPTER SIXTEEN

M AM wasn't quite as keen to leap out of bed at the crack of dawn the next day, so Ceri sneaked out early and got to the studios ahead of her again. Soon it would be the weekend though, and we could relax a bit.

I stopped off at Aunty Gwen's with some food in the morning, letting myself in by the back door as usual. 'Mael?' I called. 'You here?'

He appeared in the kitchen doorway. 'Nowhere else to go, is there?'

'There will be on Monday,' I reminded him.

'You wouldn't believe how the time drags.' He looked at his feet, suddenly. They were shoved into grotty tartan carpet slippers that would have looked old-fashioned on a ninety-year-old. Some trainers next, I decided, to go with his new jeans. 'Um –' he said, quietly.

'Um?' I busied myself putting food into the fridge. 'Um, what?'

'Well. I think there's something you ought to know.'

'Oh yeah?'

'Yeah. Remember when those boys broke in?'

'How could I ever forget! I was, like, so scared –'

'That big dog that rescued you–' he interrupted.

'I remember him. Don't mind me saying it, Mael, but

he was a lot more use than you were, but never mind that. Water under the bridge and all that. Forgiven.'

'Actually, Nia, that *was* me.'

'What was?'

'The dog. Except it wasn't a dog: it was a wolf. Sort of.'

'Yeah, right. Pull the other one; it's got bells on, Mael. Look, just forget it, all right? I have. You don't have to make up stories to get out of it. You chickened out. We all do sometimes. Forget it. No problemo!'

'I wish I could. You want to know the real reason I left home?'

'You told me that your father thought there was something wrong with you.'

'True. *That's* the problem. Why I'm here, really. I'm a – I'm – well, actually, Nia, I'm a werewolf.'

'Oh, ha ha ha! Very funny, I don't think. Look, Mael, forget it, will you? No excuses. Sometimes I feel like running away, too.'

He sighed.

I stood on tiptoe, my back to him, reaching up to put a can of beans into the top cupboard. Then I turned round again. Mael had gone.

In his place was a very large do– . . . um . . . creature.

I shut my mouth and frowned. There was definitely something I wasn't getting. It was sort of doggy, but not, like, totally. It was much too big to be a dog, and there was something about its eyes . . . They didn't have that nice, big, brown, give-me-a-pat-and-I'll-give-you-a-lick sort of expression, either. They were amber-gold, and slanted up at the corners . . .

'M-m-mael?'

It stood on its hind legs and put its huge paws on my shoulders. I sagged at the knees. It put its massive jaws close to my face. I shut my eyes. This was it. It would tear out my throat and no one would find my bloody corpse until Aunty Gwen came home from hospital, and possibly not then, if it was really hungry. A cold, wet nose nudged me. I opened my eyes. Two eyes were patiently staring into mine. Amber eyes, with flecks.

I looked at the creature. It really was him. And then the lights went out.

I came round to the sound of low growls and a cold nose prodding my face. I opened my eyes groggily and pushed the huge head away. 'Gerroff! I'm OK.' It sat back on its haunches, head on one side, waiting.

'Right.' I sat up, trying to get my head round this. 'You just – I mean, you – Mael, you turned into a wolf, yeah? You *are* a wolf, right?'

Nod.

I was sitting on the floor of my Aunty Gwenny's kitchen looking up at a wolf. A wolf that was sometimes a boy. A wolf that was maybe a boy in the day, and a wolf at night when the moon was . . .

'*You're a werewolf!*' I whispered, and felt my eyes go round and big. 'You are, aren't you?'

The wolf gave me a look that said, plain as anything, 'I just told you I was, didn't I?' It yawned, and I looked into a vast crimson cavern filled with dagger teeth.

'If there's a full moon, do you go round ripping people's throats out?'

This time, the look said, 'Duh!' which was neither a yes or a no, if you think about it.

'Look, can you turn back again? I'm beginning to feel sort of weird, talking to you.'

The huge creature padded out of the kitchen. I stood and waited, feeling totally unreal. Then he was back, Mael-the-boy, looking, like, *so normal.*

'OK. Full moon equals werewolf, right?' I knew my werewolf movies. A thought struck me. 'Hang about. It isn't a full moon now. It's broad daylight!'

'It's not all to do with full moons.'

'But isn't that the werewolf thing? Full moon, hair and fangs. And silver bullets and stuff.' Which was probably a bit tactless but he didn't seem to mind.

'Not for me. I don't need a full moon,' he repeated. 'I can change any time though a full moon means that it's harder to stop it. Sometimes I can make it happen if I concentrate hard enough. Like just now. I've got this rogue gene that's a bit unusual.'

'So any time you feel like it, you can –' I waved my hand vaguely.

'Yeah.'

'So,' I said, putting a pack of butter in the fridge, 'what you're saying is, any time, day or night, you might –'

'Mostly at night,' he mumbled.

'– *day* or *night*, you can turn into a wolf. Have I got that right?'

'Uh-huh.' He looked up at me, his amber eyes worried. 'Can I still go to school on Monday?'

I sat down suddenly on the kitchen chair. 'Let me get this

straight, right? You're a werewolf but you aren't the ordinary sort of a werewolf, yeah?'

'I s'pose.'

'Do you get any warning?'

'Yeah, I do. I get this weird feeling at the back of my neck, and I get the urge to drop onto all fours.'

'Does it hurt?'

'No – it aches a bit, after, when I change back – but that's just because I walk on two feet most of the time. But changing doesn't hurt. And clothes aren't a problem. They seem to disappear when I change and then – when I change back, I'm fully dressed. I don't know how it happens, but – good thing it does, because otherwise it might get a bit embarrassing.'

'Yeah.'

'So, can I?'

'What, school?'

'Yeah.'

I thought about it. 'If you're going to change, you always know in advance, right?'

'Right. Unless –'

'What?'

'If I lose my temper, I might just turn. Kablooey. I'm a wolf.'

'You lose your temper often?'

'Hardly ever. Only with –'

I thought I could guess. 'Your dad, right?'

He nodded.

I made a lightning decision. 'Mael, you're going to school on Monday.' I'd been giving some thought to his cover story. 'I'm going to tell them you're my long-lost cousin from

Zimbabwe, and you're staying with my aunty until your parents join you.'

His eyes were shining. 'Oh, I can't wait to get back to school. There's so much I want to learn.'

I felt guilty then, because I could have been helping him with his reading – but what with all the kerfuffle and panic at our house and then Mrs Cadwallader, I just hadn't had time. And I was going out with Ryan Saturday evening, and couldn't do it then, either. I resolved to put in some time every evening the following week. 'Right!' I gave him a big smile. 'See you Monday, bright and early, OK?'

You might think I'd accepted all this werewolf stuff much too calmly. You'd be right. I don't think my brain had quite sorted it out yet. I knew in my heart he was a werewolf, but somewhere deep inside, a little part of me was still saying, *oh, how totally, like, weird is this!*

Ceri and I both got ready for our big dates: me going to the pictures with Ryan O'Brien, she off on her party date with Pietro. She looked gorgeous, and she was so happy that she let me borrow her favourite top!

Dad gave us both a long look as we put our coats on ready to go out. 'Not too late back, now, Nia, you hear? And Ceri, who're you going out with?'

'Oh, just a friend,' she murmured.

'One of your mates, is it?'

She didn't tell him no. I wish she had.

'Are you sure you're not going to catch cold in that?' He eyed her low-necked dress. 'Haven't you got a cardi or another dress you could wear? One with a high neck?'

'Yeah, right, Dad – I'll put on a fleece, too, shall I?'

He grunted, admitting defeat. He usually did. 'Drive safe,' he muttered, and went back to his paper.

Dad had loaned Ceri the car, so she dropped me off at the cinema on the way. Ryan was already there, his Blues rugby shirt glowing in the light from the foyer.

'Have a great time, Cer,' I yelled, slamming the car door behind me. 'Take care!' I didn't only mean driving to Cardiff either. I meant: 'Take care he doesn't hurt you. Take care he doesn't break your heart!' She didn't hear, of course, and probably wouldn't have listened if she had.

Ryan's face lit up when he saw me. 'Wasn't sure you'd come,' he muttered.

'Why wouldn't I?'

'Well, I heard Mouthy Morris had a go at you.'

'And your point is?'

'Well, he was winding you up. S'embarrassing.'

'Mouthy Morris is a pain in the bum, but he's, like, so easy to ignore.'

'That's good. I threatened to thump him if he did it again.'

'You'd get suspended if you did.'

He grinned wickedly. 'Not if I did it on the rugby field. Which I would. And he knows it.'

The film had Daniel Radcliffe in it, but I couldn't tell you what it was about after the first ten minutes or so. It took that long for Ryan to slide his arm round the back of my seat, but he got there in the end. Couldn't concentrate on the film much, after that. He *might just* have kissed me – a couple of times – but I couldn't possibly comment. All I know is, he walked me home and I don't think my feet touched the pavement once.

When I let myself into the house Dad was (of course) waiting up. He said (of course), 'What time do you call this to come home?'

And I (of course) looked at my watch and said, 'Twenty past ten, Dad.'

And then he said, 'A little less cheek, young lady.'

'Sorry, Dad. Night, Dad,' and I gave him a hug. We always had this conversation if I went out out, whoever I was with.

This time, however, when he'd picked up his book and was on his way to bed, he turned in the doorway and said, 'Don't grow up too fast, Nia love, will you?'

He went upstairs, then. I did, too, but in Ceri's room. I was intending to stay awake, but it had been a long day, and I was unconscious by the time she came home. She shook me awake. 'Nia, wake up!'

I rubbed my eyes and sat up. 'You're back. Good. What happened?'

'Oh, it was amazing, Nia! Everybody was there! Matthew Rhys even, over from Los Angeles. And that bloke that's in *Pobol y Cwm*, the nice one that's after thingy, you know. And Catherine Zeta Jones was supposed to be there, but she wasn't, and – oh, Nia, everywhere I looked there was somebody famous! And I was there! Me! And I was with Pete!' She wrapped her arms round herself and spun round. 'I think I'm in love, Nia!'

Inside, I groaned. This was what I'd been afraid of. 'Are you sure?'

She grinned at me, her eyes sparkling, her cheeks pink.

'Yes. Oh, he's so lovely! He's thoughtful, and he's kind, and he opens doors for me, and introduces me to people, and he didn't leave my side all night!'

'And then you came straight home, right?' I asked.

She blushed. 'Well. Not quite. We went to his place – he's got this lush apartment in one of those converted warehouses in Cardiff Bay, and it's fantastic, Nia: you should see it!'

'And?' I demanded.

'And what?'

'I hope you only admired the view.'

She turned away then, and my heart sank.

'Oh, I did. I really, really did.'

And what was I supposed to make of that, do you suppose? I lay awake and worried for all of three minutes when I finally got into my own bed, but I was tired, and the next thing I knew it was Sunday and the smell of frying bacon was drifting up the stairwell.

CHAPTER SEVENTEEN

A FTER Sunday brunch, I decided to amble over to Aunty
Gwen's house. It was cold and a threat of winter zinged
in the air.

Mael was still up in the spare room when I arrived, so I
slung my coat down in the hall and cooked him breakfast.
He came downstairs and fell on the food like a starving –
um – wolf. I cleared the table afterwards and washed the
dishes. All très domesticated, yeah? The sun suddenly
came out, and the early chill was replaced by one of those
autumny days when the light looks clearer, somehow, and
colours brighter. Mael looked through the kitchen window.

'I'd love to go out,' he said, wistfully.

'No reason why you can't, is there?'

'Well, no – but Aunty Gwen doesn't like me to.'

'Oh, poo! Aunty Gwen's an old lady. And she's not here.
We could go for a walk if you want – Coed Arian is just up
the hill a bit.'

'Could we? Really?'

'Come on then.'

His face lit up and he put on a tatty, ancient grey
windcheater thing. I resolved to buy him a new jacket, soon.
I lifted my coat from the peg and was about to put it on
but, suddenly, Mael stiffened, and sniffed. I swear his eyes
narrowed and his ears went flat.

'What?'

'I can smell . . .' He walked round me, sniffing. 'There's something – something I don't – yes! There!' He lunged for my coat pocket and pulled out the baseball cap I'd found outside Mrs Cadwallader's shop and which I'd meant to take to the police station – but hadn't. He sniffed again, scowling. 'Where did you get this? It's them!'

'Them? Who?'

'Those boys who broke in here – the ones that mugged Gwen and stole her handbag.'

I stared at him. 'You can tell that from sniffing the hat?'

'Of course I can! I'm still a wolf inside – I retain my senses even if I don't retain my –'

'Furry bits,' I supplied. 'It was caught on a bush outside Mrs Cadwallader's shop – she got robbed the other night, and I found her. They hit her over the head, so she's in hospital too.'

Mael scowled. 'I think it's time we put a stop to this.'

'I agree. But – how?'

He grinned at me. Wolfishly . . . His eyes slanted upward, his ears seemed to lengthen, and his teeth suddenly looked Very Sharp. 'I can track them from this. We can find out where they live, and then –'

'Report them to the police?' I suggested.

'Do you think they'd believe you?'

'Why wouldn't they?'

'Think about it. What proof do you have? A hat on a bush? So what? Anyway, I have to keep my head down, remember? First we find them, Nia, then we find a way to point the police at them. Perhaps the shopkeeper –'

'Mrs Cadwallader –'

'– she might be able to describe them. And Aunty Gwen would, wouldn't she?'

I felt a grin spread across my face. 'Oh, Aunty Gwen will remember them perfectly! Come on, let's go and find them now!'

His face fell. 'I was looking forward to a walk in the woods, Nia – and anyway it would be better if we went hunting after dark. My senses work better in darkness than in daylight.'

'What, you're going to be a werewolf to track them down?'

He grinned again. 'If you've got it, use it!'

The woods were wonderful, the early autumn leaves russet and gold and amber and green, a mix of shifting hues filtering through the branches. Mael and I must have walked for over an hour before I decided we needed to head for home. For a moment, on the way back to the house, I thought I caught a glimpse of something moving in the bushes. I turned my head, but whatever it was had gone.

'What?' Mael asked.

'Nothing. Just thought I saw something.'

'Rabbit, I expect. The woods are full of them.'

'They are?'

That wolfish grin again. 'Yeah. Making me feel quite hungry –'

'Oh, yuk! Eeuw! Mael! You *can't* go around eating bunnies!'

'Wanna bet? Food is food is food if you're hungry. Until I met Aunty Gwen, I was often hungry.'

I'd forgotten how desperate he'd once been. 'Was it bad, being – well – homeless?'

'It wasn't good. The worst bit was finding somewhere to sleep. Whenever I changed, my fur would keep me warm – but once I nearly got picked up by a dog warden.'

'What about food?'

'That was hard, too. Wolf cubs are taught to hunt by their parents – I wasn't, since neither of mine was that way inclined. I don't know why I got the werewolf gene – I guess I'm a sort of throwback. Anyway, I'm possibly the worst hunter in the history of – well, werewolves. I was kidding about the rabbits – they'd hear me coming a mile off. I was hungry most of the time. Your Aunty Gwen saved me in lots of ways, Nia.'

'I s'pose she did. But it's not much of a life for you, is it? Having to hide away all the time?'

'No. But – that's going to change tomorrow, isn't it! I can't wait! School!'

It made me feel more and more guilty about bunking off. He wanted to go to school *so much*, and then there was me, sneaking out. Wasting my opportunities, right? I resolved not to miss one more day of school, ever. Well – I'd try, anyway.

'So. When are we going mugger-hunting then?'

'Tomorrow night, after school? You can come round here and I'll, you know, change, and we'll go together.'

'There's bound to be more of their tracks around Mrs Cadwallader's shop – you might be able to pick up their scent from there, too.'

'Yeah. I'll try not to rip their throats out when I meet

them! Better not hand the cap into the police station until we know where they live, though. Then you can take it in and tell them where you found it.'

I left Mael at Aunty Gwenny's house, and I went home. The rest of the family had gone to see Aunty at the hospital, and so I had the house to myself for once. Or I did until Steffan came back from Cei's, where he'd stayed on an extra night. Cei's father dropped him off at the front door. Cei was OK, but I *absolutely loathed* his dad. I couldn't wait to get rid of him.

'Ah, Nia. I can safely hand this young rogue over to his big sister, eh?' Cei's dad smiled his false smile, and I gave him an equally false one back.

'Thanks *so* much for bringing him home, Mr Mostyn-Price. Say thank you, Steffan.'

'Yeah. Thanks,' he mumbled.

Cei's father disappeared (thank goodness), and I shut the door behind him.

Steffan grinned at me and I ruffled his spiky hair.

'Don't *do* that! Ni, I'm, like, really glad our dad isn't like him. He's such a pain – he keeps trying to join in our games and stuff. But he's only pretending to be nice, and underneath you know there's this person that doesn't really like you at all.'

My little brother isn't daft. 'I know what you mean. When did you last eat?'

'McDonald's. Dinner time. But –'

'– you're starving again, yeah?'

'Yeah.'

'Me, too. Cheese on toast?' So I made us both cheese

toasties, and we sat and watched a Spiderman DVD, although Steff had seen it at least a hundred times before. We ate from plates on our laps. Lovely!

The DVD had just finished when the family came home. Ceri was still ecstatic after her party, Mam was still all happy about the acting thing, but Dad was grumpy because he'd missed *Scrum V*.

Mam flung her coat on a chair for Ceri to hang up. 'Aunty Gwen's coming home on Tuesday.'

'That's good! They're letting her out at last.'

'Well, yes – though if I'm going to be on call at the studio in Cardiff, I won't be able to run back and forth to Gwenny's all the time.' Mam sighed. 'I suppose I'll have to ring the director and back out –'

'Why can't Gwenny stay here?' Ceri suggested. Duh!

Mam sighed. 'She won't. She says she wants to go home to her own house.'

'I can quite understand that,' Dad muttered.

'Well yes, so can I. But – you know how much this part means to me, Bryn. But Gwenny was so good to me when I was little, and now I feel I ought to take care of her.'

Ceri chipped in. 'We'll all help look after her, Mam. Nia can pop in after school, I can go after work, and Dad can –'

'Your dad's going to be away on a business trip next week,' Mam said. 'Of all the times to pick, Bryn, this is possibly the very worst.'

Dad shrugged. 'Can't be helped, love. When head office calls, I've got to go.'

'I'll just have to ring Mr Goldwyn-Jones and tell him I can't do it,' Mam said sadly. 'If I can't, then I can't. I'll have

136

to sleep round at her house and you lot will have to fend for yourselves, I'm afraid.'

Which is more or less what we did anyway, wherever she slept! But I really, really didn't want Mam sleeping there, not with Mael in the house. I did what I'm good at. I thought fast on my feet. 'No, Mam. You can't pass up a chance like this. Tell you what, I'll sleep over at Aunty Gwen's, and go to school from there.'

'Oh, would you? Really? Oh, Nia, you can be so lovely when you try.'

I thought, *Thanks, Mam. I think!*

Behind her back, Ceri rolled her eyes.

'But,' Mam went on, 'you won't be here to let Steffan in when he comes home from school, so he'd better go to Gwenny's for tea every day.'

Oh, great. Mael would have to hide in the cellar.

CHAPTER EIGHTEEN

I DIDN'T get much sleep that night because the whole werewolf thing suddenly went, like, *boinnnnng!* in my head. I had this weird, detached sort of feeling, like the whole thing was so totally unbelievable. And yet at the same time I knew it was true. I'd *actually seen* Mael turn from boy to werewolf. My whole life before then had been sort of like this – blankblankblankblank. Werewolves and the Undead and Vampires and Ghouls and Zombies and stuff had been sort of there in my brain, but not real. It was good in films, and in scary books, but then switch off the telly, put down the book and forget them – Mael was making me rethink all that. He was there, real, and there was no getting away from it. Not only were there people who could change into werewolves, but there was a real one living in my aunty's house. Did that mean that the other stuff was true, too? The vampires and suchlike?

The more I thought about it, the less I felt like sleeping, and the more totally unreal the whole situation seemed. Mael had shoved the problem of Mam and Ceri right to the back burner. And I'd agreed to take this unpredictable person/creature to my school? At this point my brain went, like, 'Hahahahahahaha!' Then I started thinking about Ceri and Pietro and hoping he wouldn't hurt her, and wishing she'd tell Dad or Mam she was going out with him because keeping stuff from the people who love you isn't a good plan and . . . And so on and so on and so on. I must have fallen asleep about ten seconds before the alarm went off, so when I met Mael on the corner by Gwenny's house to take him to school, I had eyes like two holes in a Halloween mask. I know, I know, don't even try to imagine it. I also had flutterbyes under my belly button, and Wolf-Boy was pale green, so he wasn't feeling much better.

'OK?' I asked.

'K,' he mumbled.

He looked dead smart in his school stuff – a very convincing new kid. I took him to the office, hanging on to his elbow so he wouldn't panic and run. He'd faded from green to white by then, and I didn't want him disappearing on me. If I'd faced up to all the possible problems there might be in introducing a were-person to an unsuspecting high school, he had to cooperate at the very least. I thumped his arm to give him courage.

The secretary was wearing her *don't-bother-me-I'm-frightfully-busy* look, but then, she always did, first thing in the morning, what with late kids and kids that had forgotten permission forms and games kit and needed to phone home. She had to deliver a lecture to each kid (and I mean she HAD to – or it would ruin her day).

'Oh, it's you,' she said. 'What do you want?'

'Good morning!' I said, breezily. 'This is my cousin, Mael. He wants to enrol.'

She glanced at Mael. 'Oh yes? Have you got a letter from your last school?'

Mael went paler, so I jumped in. 'No. He's a migrant.'

'A what?'

'A migrant. From – um –' For a second I blanked. I'd worked all this out, but my mind went into total reverse: 'Africa.'

'Oh, really? Where's his mother? Father? Why haven't they come in to register him?'

'They're still in Zimbabwe. Mael's come home to live with my aunt.'

'Then why isn't your aunt here to register him?'

'She's in hospital.'

'Then,' said the school secretary triumphantly, 'where is he living?'

'With us,' I shot back, brain in gear and motoring again.

Her face collapsed into grumpiness. 'Well, I'll have a word with Dr Bell. Until then, I suppose he'd better stay with you for the morning at least.'

I thanked her and we scarpered. 'Success!' I crowed, waving my hand at Mael, waiting for a high five. He didn't give me one – of course – I had to demonstrate. I was *so* going to have to work on his street cred!

Double maths, first two periods (aaargh!). I took Mael into the maths room, and every eye fixed on the New Kid. Ryan's in the top set, so he didn't see me with another bloke, which was good. However, Mouthy Morris is in my set, and he was boggling a bit. So was Dubious Mike, who was shaking his head and looking – well, Dubious, but then, that's what Dubious does best.

Mael had his head down, not looking anybody in the eye (rather like a timid dog . . .), so I introduced him. My cousin, I said, from Zimbabwe.

'H'lo,' Mael mumbled.

'Not too talkative, is 'e?' Mouthy said.

'Shut up, Mouthy.' Nectar Phillips (her poor brother's called Torrent, yeah?) batted her eyelashes at Mael. 'He doesn't have to talk if he doesn't want to.'

Mael slumped into a seat AT THE FRONT of the classroom. I'd already headed for my usual seat at the back in the farthest corner, so I had to shoot back to him. 'Get up, stupid!' I hissed. 'You, like, NEVER, ever sit at the front in maths! You get picked on by the teacher. You have to hide at the back.'

'But –'

Too late. We were trapped. Sigh. I got out my books and prepared to suffer. But first I had to explain who Mael was, and where he'd come from.

Mrs Yates, maths, is possibly the MOST boring teacher in the world. She started bleating on about this train that was going from London to Glasgow at such and such a speed, and another train coming from Glasgow at such and such a speed. At what point therefore would they –'

'Crash?' Mouthy Morris muttered.

Mael was sitting bolt upright next to me. I glanced at him, afraid he was going to faint or something, but his face had eager written all over it. I mean, *maths?* Suddenly, his hand shot up in the air.

'New boy? What's your name again?'

'Mael,' he said.

'Mael, right. Yes?'

'They'd be 278.5 miles from London, miss,' he said.

Mrs Yates's jaw dropped. 'Pardon?'

'Two hundred and seventy-eight miles, miss,' repeated Mael patiently. 'Point five.'

'That's right! That's exactly *right!*' said Mrs Yates excitedly. She asked him a couple of other questions while the rest of us listened and boggled. 'At last there's a boy in this set who can do maths!' she breathed. I'd never seen her so excited.

Mael went red with pleasure. Proper little rainbow he was. After maths we had break, so we ambled into the yard. He was still grinning. 'That was great!'

'You're weird,' I told him firmly. 'So weird. Anyone who likes maths is weird.'

'But I can *do* maths! It's easy. It's logical – there's only ever one answer, and –'

'– and if you're me, it's usually the wrong one,' I finished grumpily.

Nectar Phillips sidled up to us. The eyelashes were still going like electric fans. Mael grinned at her, and she simpered back. I wanted to smack her, but there you go. Takes all sorts, and she was the other sort.

Then, behind me, Mouthy Morris's voice said, 'I'll tell Ryan you've dumped him, Nia, shall I?'

I swung round. 'What did you say?'

'I was gonna tell him anyway – I saw you in the woods with yer new bloke yesterday. Very cosy.'

'You did not!' I exploded. 'He is not my new bloke!'

'I saw you. You was walking in the woods, all snuggled up together. So if you 'aven't dumped Ry, why was you out with another bloke?'

'He's not another bloke; he's my . . .' – for a minute, I

couldn't quite remember what relationship he was supposed to be – '. . . my cousin.'

Then another voice broke in. 'Well, I was kinda Dubious when Ry said he was goin' out with you in the first place, and I'm real Dubious now, I am. Mind yew, Nia, I never had you down as a Two-Timer.'

My heart took up permanent residence in my school shoes. If Dubious Mike went to Ryan with his tales, that would probably be it. No more rugby or cinema trips. No more Ryan. The worst crime of all in our school was Two-Timing. If you were Going Out with someone, that was it. Two-Timing was Not On. Like, Totally Unacceptable.

Mael looked bewildered. He didn't have a clue. He was just trying to work out what was going on. I grabbed his sleeve. 'I'll explain later, all right?' Then the siren went for the end of break, so we went in.

I saw another side of Mael in English. Despite his brilliance at maths, he was barely able to read. He could read numbers, and do sums in his head, but words were a different kettle of fish altogether. He went bright scarlet and fumbled and flustered and misread words. Some kids started sniggering – until Mr Williams stopped them. It was horrible: Mael couldn't help it; it was just the way things were, but I was top set, and he was so not right for that! At the end of the lesson, Mr Williams came over to where we sat. 'I'm going to keep you out of your next session, Mael. I want to run some stuff past you – and see if I can find out what the problem is. I know you said you'd missed a lot of schooling, living abroad –'

Mael went pink again at this: I don't think he likes having to lie.

143

'– but it's just possible you may be dyslexic. If you are, we can help you, but anyway we've a special programme in this school to help with reading problems.'

I didn't want to leave Mael alone, but there was nothing else I could do – I had to go and suffer the Great Lakes. Sigh. Who cares? If I'm honest I didn't pay too much attention. I was worrying about what Mouthy and Dubious were going to tell Ryan. I needed to get to him first . . . As soon as geography was over, I went looking for Mael so that we could go and get lunch in the canteen together. He wasn't in Mr Williams's room, and neither was Mr W. I wandered out to the yard, where clumps of people stood, sat, lounged and flopped, same as always. Then, from round the corner of the building, I heard a familiar sound.

'Fight, fight, fight, fight –'

My stomach lurched and I felt sick. I knew, instantly, without even looking, who was fighting. I started to run.

CHAPTER NINETEEN

A MOB of shouting, excited, red-faced kids jostled around the scrappers. I shoved my way through into the centre. I was pretty sure what I was going to see: Mael in a fight. If Mael lost his temper – it could be fatal on all sorts of levels! But I couldn't work out who might have upset him. Mouthy, Dubious – or, worst case, Ryan.

It was Ryan all right but, amazingly, it wasn't Mael he was trying to hammer into the ground. *My bloke was actually having a punch-up with his best mate!*

Ryan SO isn't the school-yard punch-up type. Yet here he was, rolling in the dust with Dubious Mike! Eventually Ryan got on top, Dubious's nose was gushing red and, from the funny angle, it looked as if it might be broken.

'Go on, admit it, you bloody liar!' Ryan hissed, fist poised.

'I'm not lying!' Dubious mumbled. 'She was out with this other bloke. The new kid! Up the woods! Honest, Ry! I wouldn't lie to you! You're my best butty.'

Ryan drew back his fist.

'Don't hit him, Ryan! He's not lying – he just –'

Ryan got off Dubious Mike and stood up. He had a huge lump under his eye and his shirt was torn. He glared at me. 'It's true, then, yeah?' he asked. 'You been two-timing me?'

'No! Honestly I haven't!' I protested.

Dubious mopped his nose. 'She 'ave! I told you,' he mumbled. 'That's what mates are for, Ry. Mates tell you stuff nobody else wants to. Told you she was two-timing. I'd dump her if I was you. She's not worth it.'

'Oh, just shut up, Dubious, will you? Ryan, I wasn't doing anything wrong. He's my cousin. I'm not going out with him or anything like that! He's my cousin, honest.' I was lying, yes, but not about the essential thing. I was going to say, 'I wasn't two-timing,' but then I suddenly thought, hey, why am I even bothering? What I do is up to me, right? If Ryan doesn't trust me, then so what? If you really like someone, you need to trust them, yeah?

So, instead of trying to talk myself out of trouble, I got stroppy and scowled instead, glared back at Ryan and said, 'And so what, anyway? If you don't trust me, you can go and take a running jump. You don't own me, Ryan O'Brien, so I'll do what I want and if you don't like it, you can lump it. We've only been out twice! Who do you think you are?'

Ryan stared at me. Then he just turned and walked away.

That's it, then, I thought. *Finished. Over. Dumped.* Oooh, I felt so *miiiiserable!*

Things didn't get any better when Mably caught up with me halfway through the afternoon. Mael was off with Mr Williams again, and after that he had to go and see Dr Bell – I was going to have to weasel into that meeting somehow, to stop Mael putting his foot in it.

'Izzit true, Ni? Ryan's dumped you?'

'Didn't dump me. I dumped him. He, like, so doesn't own me.'

'Mouthy Morris is going round telling everyone he saw you with some bloke up the woods on Sunday! Were you?'

'I was just out for a walk with – with my cousin. That's all! Honest!' I hated keeping Mabs in the dark – she's my best mate after all – but she has one fault, which is a terminal inability to keep a secret. She's always accidentally letting stuff slip – not like Mouthy Morris, maliciously – but sometimes Mably's mouth is only loosely connected to her brain. There was, like, *no way* I was going to tell her about Mael. If I told her now, by the end of school there'd be riots and ructions and telly cameras and *Western Mail* reporters outside waiting to get a glimpse of the werewolf . . .

'Well, it looks bad, Nia,' she said, shaking her head and pursing her lips. 'I got to say that. Mind, I know you wouldn't two-time anybody, ever. But other people don't know you like I do, and like I said, it looks bad.'

'Don't get all wossname on me, Mabs. I don't care what it looks like. He doesn't trust me, so who cares? Anyway,' – I was starting to get indignant by now – 'twice we've been out, that's all. Who does he think he is?'

But I was whistling in the wind for all my big words, and tears were creeping up on me, and my nose was starting to run. I got out a tissue and had a blow. I made an effort to pull myself together while Mably patted me and made encouraging noises, which is what best mates are for. I might talk to Ceri about it when I got home. I would have to tell someone or bust. But right now, I had to find Mael so I could go with him to see Dr Bell – I was sure he didn't have enough confidence to pull it off by himself.

He was sitting miserably on the Suffering Chair outside her office. I knew that feeling: like being in the dentist's waiting room when you know you're going to have a filling. And you can hear the drill whining through the closed door, and the patient screaming in agony . . . OK, I exaggerate sometimes, but you get the picture. I sat beside him, and he grinned weakly at me.

'I was going to stick with you, today, but it sort of got taken out of my hands, Mael. Sorry. Have you got on OK?'

His face lit up. 'Yeah, great! Mr Williams doesn't think I'm dyslexic – it's just that I've missed so much school. I'm going to have an extra hour every day, so I can catch up. Isn't it fantastic?' His eyes were shining despite his nerves. I'll bet his nose was cold and wet, too.

'Great, Mael. Now, all we've got to do is convince Dr Bell –'

'And what is it you have to convince me of, may I ask?' I hadn't heard the Head's door open. She was standing in the doorway, arms folded, one eyebrow raised. Wish I could do that, but both mine seem to work together.

Quick, Nia, brain in gear . . . 'Erm . . . Erm . . . he should be in top set for maths! He's brilliant, Dr Bell!' I gabbled.

She lowered the eyebrow. 'Hmm. Well, I suppose you'd better come in. You too, Nia, since you seem to have appointed yourself the young man's guardian.' She stood back to let us go through first. 'Sit down, both of you.'

We sat, and I tried to look demure. Then I realised she was looking pointedly at my right wrist, on which was a friendship bracelet Mably had given me that morning. I quickly slipped it off and tucked it in my pocket.

The next half-hour was gruelling, to say the least. We'd agreed that we'd stick to the truth as much as possible. Mael didn't exactly say he was my cousin, but he did say he was staying with family – and here I butted in to say he was going to be staying with my aunt. I didn't remind Dr Bell she was still in hospital, but let her think it was another aunty. Didn't lie, did I? She seemed to swallow the Zimbabwe story whole, but then, she would, wouldn't she? I mean, no kid who's on the run is going to, like, *enrol voluntarily in a school.*

Dr Bell concluded by saying she had already been informed of Mael's remarkable talent for mathematics, and of his total lack of it in reading and writing. She smiled at him. 'Therefore top set for maths, extra help for English. We'll set you in other subjects when we've seen what you can do. You might as well stay with Nia for the time being, except for those two subjects.'

Dr Bell picked up a pile of papers and shuffled them. I understood that to mean we were dismissed, so we didn't hang about.

'Whew!' My knees were wobbly.

Mael's eyes were still shining. 'I'm in! I'm in!' he crowed. 'I'm really going to school! Isn't it great, Nia?'

'Yeah. You'll soon catch up, especially if the Williams is helping you. He's seriously cool.' The siren went for home-time. 'Free at last, yay! Come on, Mael. Let's get out of here.'

'Can't. I've got to go for a reading lesson.'

'What, now?'

'Yes.' He looked anxious suddenly. 'Is that a problem?'

'No – did I ought to wait for you, make sure you get home safely?'

He flashed me a disgusted look. 'Do you think I'm so helpless I can't find my own way home? Even if I didn't know the way, I could *smell* it, Nia!'

'Oh, right. Well –'

'Don't worry. I'll be fine. Meet you tomorrow, same place?'

'OK – hey, aren't we going after the muggers tonight?'

'Yeah.'

'I'll come over as soon as I've had my tea, all right?'

'And Aunty Gwen should be home tomorrow – that'll be great. I've really missed her, Nia.'

Which was when I realised. When Gwenny came home, *someone* was going to have to break the news that her secret were-lodger was going to school these days . . . And guess who that was going to be! Ah well, I'd just have to bite the bullet, right? (No, not a silver one.)

Steffan was waiting on the doorstep when I got back, so I let him in, made us both a cheese sandwich to keep us going, and then got down to some revision homework. Yes! Me! Homework!

According to the experts, the best way is to study really hard for forty minutes and then take a twenty-minute break . . . So I took the twenty-minute break first, and had a bit of a sob about losing the love of my life after only two dates. I knew I'd feel better when Ceri came home and I could have a moan to her. Once I'd had a really good bawl, I took off my uniform and put on jeans and a T-shirt and got down to it. I was still working when I heard the back door open and someone come in. 'That you, Ceri?' I called.

'No. It's me.' Dad.

'Hi, Dad. Just doing a bit of studying, all right? Be down later.'

There was a pause. 'Studying? Did you say *studying*? Am I in the right house?'

'Oh, ha ha ha, very funny. Not.' I got my head down and tried to remember anything I'd ever known about the geography of Canada.

A bit later I closed the books with a groan. Some of the stuff I was revising I couldn't remember doing the first time round!

I heard Mam come in and start telling Dad all about her day (she obviously hadn't run into Ceri at the studios yet, so that was a blessing). I was packing my schoolbag ready for the next day, thinking about going over to Aunty Gwen's that night and taking off after the muggers, and trying not to think about losing Ryan O'Brien, when Mam let out a blood-curdling shriek downstairs.

I took the stairs about six at a time. She was sitting in the kitchen, clutching the morning copy of the *Western Mail*, her eyes squinched shut.

'What?' I said, puffing. 'Has somebody died?'

'Worse!' she exclaimed. 'It's Ceri –' Mam handed me the *Western Mail* . . .

CHAPTER TWENTY

Dad tottered in, looking a bit bleary from 'resting his eyes' over the crossword. 'What?' he mumbled.

'You may well ask!' Mam said.

'I *am* asking, love,' he said patiently.

'It's Ceri. She's Let Us Down.'

Dad sat down wearily at the kitchen table. 'You want to start at the beginning, my lovely?'

Mam shoved the *Western Mail* under his nose. 'Look!'

He unfolded the crumpled paper and scanned it. 'What? The Assembly getting its knickers in a twist again?'

'*Page seven!*' Mam tossed her hair. '*Picture, top right.*' She was hissing. Not a good sign.

Dad glanced at her over the top of his glasses, and turned to page seven. 'What? Oh – WELSH HEART-THROB PIETRO ANNIGONI JONES OUT ON THE TOWN? Is that it? The gossip column? Is that significant somehow?'

'*Reeeeead the aaaarticle!*'

Dad sighed and started reading. '*Pietro Annigoni Jones, seen last night at a reception, with a mystery companion. Who is the new love in the Italian superstar's life?*'

At that point, my stomach wobbled violently, and I started to feel sick.

Dad tossed the paper on the table. 'Honestly! Does anyone care? Oh – is he the one that's in this TV thing you're doing?' He stopped suddenly, and frowned. 'Not jealous, are you?'

Mam rolled her eyes. 'Of course I'm not jealous! *Look at the picture!* Are you blind? Look, will you!' She shoved the paper back at him.

Dad picked it up and looked. I peeped over his shoulder, and there, on page seven of the *Western Mail*, all done up to the nines and looking gorgeous, was my big sister. She was gazing adoringly up at Pietro Annigoni Jones, who wasn't looking down at her but flashing his gleaming choppers at the paparazzi, instead.

Dad stiffened, suddenly. 'That's –'

'Ceri!' Mam said. 'Our daughter! Out with that, that pseudo-Italian Welshman!'

Dad cleared his throat. 'And why not? She's entitled to date anyone she pleases, isn't she? She's legally an adult.'

'She may be an adult, Bryn, but she lied to us.'

'She *what?*'

'She went behind our backs. She said she was going out with a friend last night. I won't put up with it, Bryn!'

'She didn't lie. He obviously is a friend. As for putting up with it, I don't see as we've got much choice,' Dad said reasonably, and I winced. What *is it* about blokes? Disagreeing with her when she was in this mood? Stand by for fireworks! 'She is,' he repeated, 'legally an adult.'

Mam exploded. 'That's not the point. What's she getting up to if she can't tell us who she's going out with? Where did she meet him, anyway? He's playing the detective in this drama I'm going to be in. And another thing – what time did she get home?'

I could have told her, but I thought it might be safer not to mention that it was around four o'clock in the morning.

'Again, my lovely, she's legally an adult, and she doesn't have a curfew. As to where she met this Pietro What's-'is-name, what you don't know is, as a matter of fact –'

Oh, it was just as well I was standing behind him at that point and I could dig him really hard in the back to shut him up. I *knew* it was a mistake, letting him in on Ceri's secret! Fortunately, he suddenly realised what he was about to say, took the hint (or rather the poke in the back) and shut up.

'As a matter of fact *what?*'

'Ceri's an adult, Mam,' I supplied.

'Shut up, Nia. Nobody asked you. And don't think *you're* ever going to go gallivanting around like she does, my girl!'

'But she can if she wants to! And *I'm* not doing anything!' I protested. *Yet* I thought.

Suddenly I heard the unmistakeable sound of a pair of high heels tapping up the path. Ceri. Luckily I was on Mam's wrong side right then, so it was an excellent excuse for me to do a teenage strop, which I do so seldom that I think I really ought to fake one occasionally, like now, so I don't get out of practice. I stamped out, slammed the kitchen door behind me – and shot out the front door to intercept my sister, who was standing there, key in hand. I grabbed her arm and hustled her round the corner.

'What? Gerroff, Nia!'

'Ceri, she's found out about you and Pietro whatsit.'

'How? Did you tell her?'

'Don't be daft. Of course I didn't. You only got your photo splashed all over the *Western Mail*, didn't you!'

She went white, then pink, then white again. 'What am I going to say? What can I do?'

'If I were you, Ceri, I'd make myself scarce until she cools down a bit. And try to think of some excuse that won't set her off again.'

'She can't tell me what to do!' Now Ceri was getting mad. 'How dare she? I'm an adult. I can see whoever I like! I'm going to tell her . . .'

'Yeah. I know. But if you go in there with all your guns blazing and say that, sooner or later – and probably sooner – she's going to ask you where you met him, isn't she? And what are you going to say then?'

'Oh. Yeah. See what you mean. Oh, Nia, this is all so complicated! You're so lucky: you haven't a care in the world, and all this is on my shoulders.'

That's all you know, Ceri, I thought. *I've been publicly Dumped and Totally Humiliated by the love of my life for something I didn't do; I've got a werewolf accompanying me to school; I'm living like I've got a time bomb tucked in my knickers and you say I haven't a care?*

'That's me, Cer,' I muttered. 'Not a cloud in my sky. Now, you get yourself lost and I'll try to calm Mam down.'

'I'll be round Siân's if you want me, all right? Her mam won't mind if I move in for a couple of nights. Tell me when you think it's safe to come home.'

'OK. Better catch the early train tomorrow, mind.'

'Thanks, Nia.' She suddenly grabbed and hugged me. 'You're a good kid, all things considered. Love you.'

I couldn't remember her ever saying that before, nor me to her. But, I realised suddenly: it was true. She wasn't only my sister these days; she'd become a mate. After years of scrapping, we'd stopped. Well, temporarily, at least!

I watched her scuttle off, then let myself in the back door, quietly. Dad was sitting in the kitchen, the *Western Mail* still spread out on the table in front of him. He wasn't poring over Ceri's picture – he was reading the rugby page, which was sort of comforting. Mam had disappeared, and I could hear Steffan's computer game-thingy bleeping away upstairs. All was, on the surface at least, normal.

Dad looked up. 'Where's Ceri?' he whispered.

'She's gone round Siân Jones's for the night. Sorry I had to thump you – but you were going to tell Mam Ceri's secret, weren't you?'

'Yes.' He looked shamefaced. 'I was. You were right, Nia – I can't keep secrets from her, can I?'

'You never could, Dad. But that's just one of the reasons why I love you.' I kissed the top of his head. 'Where's Mam?'

'Taken herself off to bed. She says she's never going to forgive me for siding with Ceri.' He ran his hand over what was left of his hair. 'I mean, what am I going to do? She's upset enough by Ceri going behind her back with this Pietro bloke.'

'Yeah. But you can understand why Ceri doesn't want Mam to find out about her acting, and if she'd told you about Pietro, she'd have had to say where she'd met him, wouldn't she? I don't think she meant to go behind your backs, not really.'

'I suppose. But it's not good, secrets in a family.'

Dad, Steffan and I phoned out for a pizza, a big one, and ate it glumly round the kitchen table. Mam stayed upstairs, and Dad didn't say much. We'd finished eating and I was stacking the plates in the dishwasher, when Steffan suddenly burst out: 'Are you and Mammy going to get a divorce?' His face was red and his eyes were teary.

Dad looked up, startled. 'Good grief, Steffan! Of course not! Where'd you get that daft idea?'

'Well, you and Mammy were arguing, and Mammy's all upset!'

It would have been funny if it hadn't been so tragic. Dad gathered my little brother into his arms. 'Don't worry, Steffan. Mammy and I are going to stay married for ever and ever. Once your mam finishes this acting thing, it will be all over, I promise. She's just a bit stressed out at the moment. It's a bit like you and Spiderman. You aren't really able to leap tall buildings at a single bound, are you?'

Steffan thought about it, then shook his head. 'S'pose not.'

'You're sensible enough to know it's a sort of dream, right? Well, Mammy's got a dream, too: she thinks she's going to be a famous actress. I really don't think it's going to happen, but until she knows that too, we have to be very kind, and let her go on believing. Just like –'

'Like you pretend I'm Technoman sometimes. And Nia, if she's in a good mood.'

'Yes. That's just it. So,' Dad finished, 'you can go to bed and not worry about us getting a divorce, because it isn't going to happen. No way, Hosay!'

Steff sniffed. 'Honest?' And then added quickly, looking sideways at Dad, 'But I can't go to bed yet. I'm too stressed.'

'Bed!' ordered Dad.

We were back to normal. Steffan did go to bed, and when we were alone, I slumped in a chair opposite Dad and blew out a huge sigh.

'Oh, what a tangled web we weave,' he began.

'– when first we practise to deceive,' I finished.

'What are we going to do, Nia?' My dad, asking me for advice!

'Well, we wing it, Dad. No use meeting trouble halfway. She'll find out about Ceri soon enough, and we'll handle it then. But Dad – pleasepleaseplease be careful what you say. If Mam finds out about the acting now, when she's all upset over Ceri and Pietro, it's going to be ten times worse. At least.'

'You're right. You're quite sensible for a teenager, Nia.'

'Someone's got to be, in this family.'

'What about this Pietro lad, then? Him and Ceri. What do you think?'

I shrugged. 'Dunno, Dad. Like you said, Ceri's legally an adult. She's got a right to see anyone she likes.'

Dad frowned. 'I didn't necessarily mean it though, Nia! She's my daughter, after all, and I –'

*

It wasn't until I'd got to bed an hour or so later that I remembered I was a Dumped Person. And that I'd promised to go Mugger-hunting with Mael that evening. And Aunt Gwenny would be home tomorrow from hospital, which might put a spanner in the works.

CHAPTER TWENTY-ONE

MAEL wasn't a happy were-person. 'I thought you were coming over last night.'

I felt really guilty: he didn't have enough confidence in himself to cope with me not turning up. 'I was, and I'm really sorry – but we had a family crisis. Honestly, Mael, I'm so sorry. Can we go tonight instead?'

'But won't Gwenny be coming home tonight?'

'Yes, but I'll ring the hospital later to check,' I said. 'It's not a problem. I'm going to be sleeping here at Aunty Gwen's for a couple of nights to make sure she's OK. We can wait until she's asleep and sneak out.'

His face lit up. 'Oh, great.'

'You'll need to be a bit careful, mind – my brother's coming round after school every day while I'm staying at Aunty Gwen's, and he finishes earlier than we do. You might have to hide in the cellar until he goes home.'

He shrugged. 'I've done it before.'

'I know, but –' It suddenly seemed awful that he was forced to hide away from everybody.

'Anyway, what was the crisis?'

'Just family stuff, you know.'

He shook his head. 'No, I don't.'

What was the matter with me? He didn't have a clue

what a family crisis was like – he'd never had a proper family, had he? So I filled him in on the whole Ceri-Mam-Pietro story.

Mael was silent for a brief, stunned moment. It was a lot to take in.

'Come on,' I said, looking at my watch. 'We're going to be late for school!'

Naturally, the first person I set eyes on in the yard was Ryan O'Brien. He ignored me. OK. If that was how he wanted it, then that's how it was. If he didn't trust me, then that was it. What did I care?

Well, quite a lot actually. I felt that burny feeling at the back of my eyes that warns a person to get a tissue out, quick. But I wasn't going to cry in front of him – or behind his back, either. I sniffed. I'd forgotten about Mael and his Instincts.

'What's the matter?' he said.

'Oh, nothing.'

'Yes, there is. What?'

'Oh – I was going out with this boy. Ryan O'Brien. And I'm not any more. End of story, all right?'

'Not all right. What happened?'

'He thought I was two-timing, that's all.'

'What's two-timing?'

He really didn't know anything, did he? 'It's when you're going out with someone, a couple, like, and then you go out with someone else at the same time.'

'Oh. Were you?'

'Nope.'

'Then why would he think you were?'

160

'Because someone with a very big mouth saw you 'n' me together and told him.'

'You and me? Saw us when?'

'Up the woods. When we went for that long walk. Mouthy Morris saw us. Can we drop it now?'

'But that's awful! This Mouthy person saw us walking together, and he told what's-'is-name –'

'Ryan.'

'And Ryan didn't believe you when you told him the truth?'

'Obviously not, because he's gone and dumped me. Look, Mael, drop it. Please? It's not important.'

'It is if you're upset.'

Fortunately, Nectar Phillips sidled up then, and offered Mael a prawn-cocktail crisp and batted her eyelashes, handily distracting him. He's a bloke. What can I say?

When the siren went, I took Mael into the art room with me. Mrs Richards's eyes lit up when she saw him: there's nothing she likes better than testing out a new kid – I think she's hoping to discover the next Rembrandt or something. But she was in for a disappointment.

'Hmm,' she muttered when she came to see his work. 'Interesting use of colour. Are you colour-blind, by any chance?'

'I don't know.'

Mrs Richards pointed to a large red leaf he'd painted. 'What colour is that?'

'Um. Leaf-coloured.'

She pointed to a green splodge. 'And that?'

'Um – red?'

'I think we can safely say you're colour-blind. Ah well. Never mind.'

As we filed out of art and headed for history, Mael whispered, 'What's colour-blind?'

'It means you can't see colours right. My Uncle Dilwyn is colour-blind, and he always has to have his socks checked by my Aunty Cath before he goes out in case they're two different colours.'

'Oh. Then I'm colour-blind, I suppose. I don't think I see colours at all. Just – well, I don't know. Sort of shades of the same colour.'

'That's what dogs see, apparently –' And maybe wolves, too? Interesting, that!

Mael had his extra reading lesson at lunchtime instead of after school so we walked home together. Unfortunately we left school at the same time as Mouthy Morris, who smirked irritatingly, and mouthed 'two-timer!' at me. I wanted to make an extremely rude gesture, but I can be a lady sometimes. Just not often.

I rang the hospital when we got home and the nice doctor confirmed that Aunty Gwen would be discharged later on. Mael did a bit of tidying and I found some stewed apple in the freezer and made a crumble. We'd have corned beef and chips to start. Not exactly *Masterchef*, but tasty, especially with a dollop of pickle (the corned beef, I mean, not the apple crumble).

It was nearly six o'clock before a taxi pulled up outside, and Aunty Gwen got shakily out, carrying a large plastic bag with HOSPITAL PROPERTY written on it in big black letters. Mael and I rushed out to help her up the path.

'What are you doing out here?' she whispered to Mael. 'Get back inside: someone might see you!'

Aunty Gwenny so wasn't going to be happy when she found out he'd not only been outside, but had also been to school! I sensed storms ahead.

We wheeled her in, and she exclaimed with pleasure about how tidy the room was, and sat down and noshed her way through the corned beef and chips.

When she'd finished, she wiped her mouth and burped happily. 'That was so nice after all the hospital food!'

Mael cleared away, and then we washed up together while Aunty Gwen settled down in front of the telly with a cup of tea. I went upstairs and made up a bed in the third bedroom for myself, and by the time I got downstairs Mael had finished in the kitchen and was lying on the rug in front of the telly.

'Now, you children,' Aunty Gwen started, and I knew from the tone of her voice that this was where it was all going to start . . .

I tried to deflect her. 'Children? We're not children!'

'Oh yes you are. You may be a teenager, Nia, but you're still a child to me. And as for you, Mael, I can't have you going outdoors and showing yourself to the neighbours.'

'Why not, Aunty?' I asked.

'Because they'll start to wonder why I've got a young boy staying with me, won't they? You know the neighbours round here – a lot of lace-curtain twitchers.'

'Then we'll just have to think up a cover story, won't we?'

Mael was lying very still with his eyes shut.

'What? Lie? I don't think so, Nia. That wouldn't be very nice, would it, lying to my neighbours!'

'Tell them he's your nephew come to stay.'

'Why would a nephew move in with me? I'm an old woman.'

'Because his mother's dead and there's nobody else to look after him?'

'What if someone went to Social Services about him? I might lose my pension!'

'No, you wouldn't. In fact, you might even qualify for Child Benefit or something. Until he leaves school anyway.' Oops. Meant to break that gently . . .

'School! Don't be silly, Nia. He's not going to school!'

'Yes I am, Aunty.' Mael sat up. 'I've been twice now. I've got a uniform and everything. It's great.'

'But you can't!' she wailed.

'Yes I can.'

'But – what if you lose your temper and – and –' Aunty Gwen glanced at me, and stopped.

'It's all right. I know exactly what Mael is. But even werewolves need an education.'

'You know? How?'

'Oh, Aunty, you must have guessed I'd find out.'

She stared at me. 'Aren't you frightened?'

'Of Mael? No, why should I be? He's my friend.'

She bit her lip and thought. Then, 'No, it's not possible. What if he accidentally changes and someone's looking?'

'I won't. I promise. Whatever anyone does or says to me, I promise I won't change. I can control it, Aunty Gwen. All I have to do is not lose my temper, ever, while I'm at school.

Oh, please don't stop me! I really, really need to go – I'm going to have to find a job some time and, if I can't read or write, how am I going to get one?'

'Why do you need a job? I told you, when I'm gone you can have this house, and whatever money I've got is yours.'

'And THAT would make the neighbours talk, wouldn't it!' I butted in. 'Aunty Gwen, just stop and think a minute – Mael's registered in school now, and he's got his uniform and everything. I used some of your money to buy it. We got round the problem of where he's come from. You've got to let him keep going, Aunt Gwenny. I'll look after him, I promise. I'll stick to him like green on grass. Honest I will.'

Aunty Gwen chewed her lip. 'I don't know what to say. You don't understand properly, Nia.'

'I *do* understand. I know he's a werewolf, Aunty Gwen. It's just a little gene problem. Nothing that can't be overcome.'

She still looked doubtful. 'You know what would happen if you *turned* where people could see you, don't you? Remember Our Aelfryn!'

'Our Aelfryn?' I said. 'Who's Our Aelfryn?'

Aunty Gwen glanced up at one of the black-and-white photos. 'That's Our Aelfryn. The little short fat one in the middle. He's all bundled up.'

'*What* happened to Our Aelfryn?' I croaked.

'Well, he was a – well, not a werewolf, exactly, but –'

'But what?'

'You know – like Mael, only he was a vampire, not a werewolf. Terrible trouble with sunlight he had, but if he was well wrapped up, and wore sunglasses and lots of thick, thick pancake make-up, he was fine. Made him look a bit peculiar, but it worked well enough for him to go out in daytime on special occasions. Little outings and things, you know.'

Gulp. Werewolves. Vampires. What next? Zombies? No, forget that. I didn't want even to *think* about un-dead people with bits dropping off all over the place. 'What happened to him?'

'*O, Duw*! Tragic, it was. Took him out on a family picnic, and – '

'What?' Mael and I said together.

'Some of the kids pulled off his hat and scarf . . . Only joking, but –'

'Ouch!' I said. 'And?'

Aunty Gwen nodded sadly. 'Crumbled to dust and blew away. Things were never the same again . . .'

CHAPTER TWENTY-TWO

I JUST sat and sort of boggled. All these Creatures of the Night (no offence, Mael) popping so casually into the conversation. 'So, Aunty Gwen,' I said, when I'd got my breath back a bit. 'Like, what *is* it with you and all these – um – Different People?'

Aunty Gwen sipped her tea. 'I don't really know, *cariad*. I met my first one when I was ten – he was like you, Mael dear, except he only changed when there was a full moon, bless him! Such a dear, sweet boy. I suppose it just sort of went on from there. I like to think of myself, and this house, as a kind of underground railway.'

'What? Like the Tube in London?'

'No. Like in the southern states of America when there was slavery.'

Then I understood, sort of. I said I liked history, didn't I? Well, I love historical fiction, and I'd read this book all about these people who lived in the southern half of North America, who set up safe houses for black slaves escaping from their owners and running away to the north, where they could be free. That was called the Underground Railroad. 'So,' I said, slowly, 'you take in vampires and werewolves. What do you do with them?'

'I don't *do* anything, Nia. I just give them a sort of safe place to be. Sometimes they're just travelling through; sometimes – like Our Aelfryn and Mael – they stay. They're very interesting people, usually – especially the vampires. Some of them have been around for *so long* and they know such a lot of lovely gossip!' She sort of hugged herself with delight. 'You know, there was one a while ago – before you came, Mael, dear – who actually lost his head in the French Revolution!'

'Eeeuw! Was he headless, or what?'

'Well, of course not, dear! Luckily they buried all his bits together, so he didn't have to go looking for his head or anything. They didn't know he was a vampire, of course; they thought he was just another aristocrat, so they didn't think to bury him at a crossroads with a stake through his heart. He was up and about in no time! A bit cross, but none the worse for wear.'

Mael was sitting up now, interested. 'So I'm not the first?'

'No, lovely boy! Not a bit of it! You'd be the, oh, let me see now, the sixth – no, the seventh were-person I've had through here. And goodness knows how many vampires!'

'Were-person? You mean there are lady werewolves?'

'Of course! Adam and Eve, lovely girl, always one of each!'

'Where did they go? After, I mean?'

Aunty Gwen shrugged. 'Don't know, Nia. I gave them a bed for the night – that's why there are extra-thick curtains *and* shutters in your room, Mael dear, so you can get a good night's sleep even if there's a full moon – or a good day's sleep, if they're vampires of course – and then they left as soon as it was safe. Never one as young as Mael.' She reached out and patted him. 'He's my baby, really.'

If anyone else had heard Aunty Gwen talking, they probably would have phoned for an ambulance. I was boggling a bit, mind.

Then my aunt got back on track. 'But this business of you going to school, Mael, I'm still not sure about that, no, not at all.'

'One day, Aunty Gwen,' Mael said softly, 'I'd like to get married and have a family –'

Cubs! I thought.

'– and I'm going to have to earn a living. I'll need to read and write to be able to do that.'

'And,' I added, 'he'll need to be in the system, won't he? He'll need a National Insurance number, stuff like that. We've somehow got to organise that for him.'

'Oh, that's easy enough, Nia!' Aunty Gwen said. 'We know his name. All we need to do is get a copy of his birth certificate, and then we can get anything he likes. Even a passport if he wants.'

'Really?' Mael's face lit up. 'You mean I could go places?'

'Yes, of course you *could* – but I really don't think it's a good idea.'

Mael knelt in front of her, removed her cup of tea and held her hands. 'I can control it, Aunty Gwen, honestly I can. You don't need to worry. I'll be fine, I know I will. Anyway, Nia's looking after me – she won't let me get into any trouble.'

'Right!' I agreed.

Aunty Gwen sniffed. 'And who's going to look out for *her*, I'd like to know?'

I suppose she had a point there!

By the time Aunty Gwen went to bed, she'd come round,

if reluctantly, to the idea of Mael going to school. I wasn't in the slightest bit worried. I thought we'd be just fine.

Which just goes to show how much I knew! I tucked Gwenny up with a sleeping pill and a cup of hot chocolate, and we waited until she'd dropped off.

Then Mael and I sneaked downstairs. By that point, I'd almost forgotten about our mission.

'Bring some paper and a pencil, Nia,' Mael suggested.

'What for?'

'In case you need to write anything down . . . like an address or something.'

'Oh, yeah, right.' I found a pen and an old envelope and stuffed them in my jacket pocket. I lifted Mael's coat off the hook.

He shook his head. 'Don't need that.'

'But it's freezing out!'

'Not if you've got a fur coat!'

'Oh. Yeah, right.'

He got the baseball cap from where he'd hidden it, and handed it to me. I stood holding the cap expectantly, waiting for him to wolf up. I'd never seen anyone change into a werewolf before, and I was interested.

'Um. D'you mind turning round, Nia?'

'What? Oh, *right!* Sorry, Mael!' I obediently turned my back, and stood listening to various odd noises as he transformed. It was a bit frustrating. I'd have really liked to watch him change. On telly they did it roaring and writhing, slowly morphing into great hairy, ugly beasts, but when Mael did it, the process seemed much quieter, like someone changing into their bathers on the beach.

At last I heard a short whine. I turned, and there was Werewolf Mael, his shoulders as high as my waist. His coat was dark and rough and he gazed up at me with great almond amber-gold eyes. He really was an extremely handsome creature. I got this *terrible urge* to tickle him behind his ears and scratch his chest – but I thought I'd better not.

'Ready?' I asked instead. The great head inclined, and he stretched his neck to sniff at the baseball cap in my hand. He growled, a low-toned, resonant rumble emanating from deep in his chest. It made me break out in goose pimples, honest it did.

I started to open the front door, but Mael sideswiped it shut with his tail, turned and headed for the cellar door.

'Oh, right. Better not go out the front in case the neighbours see?'

He glanced over his shoulder and raised an eyebrow as if to say, *stupid!* I opened the door and we headed down the cellar steps and out the back gate into the lane. Round the corner, Mael put his nose to the ground and sniffed his way down the road towards Mrs Cadwallader's corner shop. While he was on the trail, his great plumy tail hung low, and periodically he'd growl, his lips drawn back from strong, savage white teeth. I knew he was a wolf – but I imagine anyone seeing him would think he was just an exceptionally large Alsatian dog . . . probably.

He suddenly took off, streaking round the corner, me panting along behind him. 'Wait for me, Mael!' I wheezed. 'I can't run as fast as you!'

He slowed obligingly, waiting on the corner for me to catch up, then padded down a narrow street of terraced houses, each with its own tiny front garden. Suddenly he stopped. He snarled and huffed, softly.

'What?'

He nudged my coat pocket.

'Oh, right.' I took out the paper and pen, and wrote down the house number – 23 – and the street name – Cwmparc Street. 'That's it! We've got him!'

Mael gave me a patient look, and I realised – almost as if he were speaking to me – that we didn't have him at all. All we had was a hat, the owner of which lived in this particular house.

'How are we going to find out if it's the same yob that lives there?' I asked. I could hardly knock on the door and ask if he owned the hat, could I? Mael answered by padding across the road and settling down under a bush in a front garden opposite.

'I can't wait there!' I complained. 'Someone might see me and call the police.'

Mael jerked his head as if to say, *go home then*.

'No way am I going home without you! I'm staying.'

He gave the equivalent of a wolfish shrug. So I huddled in beside him, in the shadow of someone's garden wall, hoping that no one would come out of the front door to put the cat or the milk bottles out – *especially* not the cat.

'What if he doesn't come out?'

Mael looked at me, and I realised the house was dark, and there were no chinks of light showing around curtains or telly flickers. There was nobody home, so we were waiting for someone to come back, not go out.

We sat and waited. And waited. My feet were blocks of

ice, and my nose was starting to drip. I huddled closer to Mael, who was warm and seemed perfectly comfortable. I peered at my watch in the light of a street lamp and saw that the hands had crept round to three in the morning. I yawned.

And then Mael's ears pricked up and he tensed, long before I heard the sound of soft-shod feet coming down the road. A shadowy figure walked up the dark street, and slipped in through the gate of the house opposite. He was carrying a heavy-looking bag. I recognised him immediately as the other one, not Dwayne. The one whose name I didn't know.

'That's him, Mael!' I whispered. *'It's him! I bet he's been breaking and entering again!'*

Mael rumbled, so softly it was more of a vibration than a growl.

'Gotcha!' I muttered. We waited until the front door closed behind him, and then I stood up, all my leg muscles cramping and aching. 'Now what?'

Mael padded out the gate and set off in the direction of Aunty Gwen's house. Mystified, I followed. Weren't we going to do anything? Wasn't he going to break in and rip the thug to shreds? What was the point of tracking him down if we weren't going to marmalise him for what he'd done to Aunty Gwen and Mrs Cadwallader?

Back at Aunty Gwenny's, I turned my back while Mael changed. When I turned round, he was back in jeans and sweatshirt.

'What was the use of that?' I asked indignantly. 'So we know where he lives! Like, big deal! He's got away scot-free!'

Mael grinned. 'No he hasn't,' he said. 'I've got a plan!'

'Oh yeah? What?'

'I need to think about it a bit more. Anyway, I'm starving. I always get hungry after I've changed. What is there to eat?'

Now that he mentioned it, I was a bit peckish myself. I found a hunk of cheddar and some crisps and we got stuck in.

When we'd finished, Mael yawned. 'I'm totally shattered. We need to get some sleep or we'll never get up for school tomorrow.' He glanced at the clock. 'It's gone four o'clock, and we've got to get up early to lay out Aunty Gwen's breakfast before we leave for school. It's good that I don't need a lot of sleep. It's one of the perks of being a werewolf.'

'Lucky you. I, on the other hand, am a zombie if I don't get my eight hours minimum.' And what I was going to get was about three hours maximum from the look of things. Even if he told me his plan I probably wouldn't remember a word of it in the morning.

I dug my electric toothbrush from my backpack and did my teeth, hoping Aunty Gwen was deeply enough asleep that the low buzz wouldn't disturb her. I tissued off my eye make-up (always do this or you'll have bad skin and wrinkles) and then fell into bed. They say that eating cheese at night gives you nightmares – but if I had any, I didn't remember them.

CHAPTER TWENTY-THREE

I GROANED, hauled the pillow over my head and tried to pretend I hadn't heard the alarm clock. I was just dozing off again in my warm little cocoon when the bedroom door opened, and the mattress – with me clinging to the edges – was dragged off the bed and dumped on the floor.

'Ow! Stop it, Mael!'

If he'd had a tail right then, he'd have been wagging it. 'Come on, dormouse. We've got stuff to do and places to go.'

'What, like school you mean?'

'Yeah, like school. And sort out breakfast for Aunty Gwen – and I bet your homework's not up to date.'

I groaned. 'There's only history, and that can wait until tomorrow.'

'You should do it the same night you get it.'

I opened a bleary eye and glared. 'Will you listen to yourself? You sound like my dad! Get a life, Mael!' I pulled the duvet over my head and prepared to go back to sleep even if I was on the floor, but he wasn't having any. He grabbed my feet and hauled me out from under. I know when I'm beaten. I trudged to the bathroom, slammed the door, which made me feel better, and showered. Ah well. It woke me up a bit.

Downstairs, I got myself on the right side of a bowl of

cornflakes, some toast and peanut butter and a cup of tea, and felt I might possibly survive. Mael had already eaten, and was getting Aunty Gwen's breakfast ready. She was still asleep when we left for school (probably catching up on all she'd missed in hospital), so we crept out of the house and shut the door quietly behind us.

I sneezed in the chilly air, felt in my pocket for a tissue and found the crumpled bit of paper with the address on it from last night. I slipped it into my homework diary where it wouldn't go astray. Don't know how much good it was going to do us, mind. All we had was the mugger's address: without a name to go with it, it didn't mean much.

'Mael?'

'Mmm?'

'You said last night you had a plan, right? To fix the muggers?'

'Ho yes!'

'And?'

'If we know where he lives, we can point the police in the right direction, yeah?'

'No. Won't work.'

'Why?'

'Well, we don't know his name, do we?'

'No, but –'

'If we don't know his name, we can hardly go and tell the police about him, can we? We can't just walk into the cop shop and say, "There's this guy. He lives by there. Don't know his name, but he's the one who mugged my aunty. Go get 'im!" Can we?'

'Well no, but –'

'So we haven't got anything, really, have we?'

'We've got the baseball cap. That's a clue. We know it's his, because I can smell him on it.'

'Oh yeah, right! We can just swan into the cop shop and say, "Oh, Nice Mr Policeman, sir, my friend's a werewolf, and he's sniffed out the person that owns this hat and he's the one that mugged my aunty and we know where he lives."'

'Oh. Right.' His face fell, and I felt a bit guilty for taking his dog biscuit away, so to speak.

'Perhaps if we can find out his name . . .'

'Phone book? We've got the address, after all.'

'You need a name to find an address and number – and no way can we search the entire phone book for the address!'

'There must be some way. Keep thinking.'

I didn't see Ryan when I got to school, which was a relief, although I was bound to bump into him sooner or later, because we had PSHE together last period. I wasn't looking forward to it. I was trying to analyse how I felt about him: I still really liked him, but he didn't trust me, and took Mouthy's word (and Dubious's) over mine, which wasn't fair, and he was taking me for granted after two dates. At least Mael wouldn't be in the lesson (extra reading), which was a relief. Better all round if those two stayed well apart.

Mael and I had an IT class together in the morning. I didn't mind that, except when we were doing spreadsheets and bar charts and pie charts and stuff – that was mathematical, and, for me, Mathematical+Anything = Boring^2. I didn't mind doing databases, which was a bit more useful for people who like their facts organised. Databases are cool. I suddenly had an idea and I put up my hand.

'Nia?' Mr Powell was OK for a teacher – he wasn't entirely sarky, only sometimes if someone really annoyed him. Then his tongue could slice raw steak at twenty paces.

'Sir, if I wanted to find out someone's name, and I only had their address, how would I go about doing it? Is there anything on the internet that could do that?'

'Good question, Nia. Anyone got any ideas?'

Everyone went quiet – which might mean they were thinking, or it might mean they were, like, totally brainless. First, one of the Bighead Brigade stuck his hand up. 'Sir, sir, Mr Powell, sir – what about a reverse phone directory?'

'Good idea, Melvyn. There are plenty on the internet, but it would cost you money to access it. There's actually an easier way if you only want local addresses and people. Any ideas?'

SG put up his hand. SG stands for SuperGeek, which sounds insulting, but it isn't. SuperGeek is one of those kids that are so good at everything, and so nice with it, you can't possibly dislike them! If it had just been 'Geek', now THAT would have been insulting!

'The electoral roll, sir?'

Mr Powell grinned happily. 'Would you like to explain the electoral roll, SG?' The SG nickname has caught on, even with the staff.

'The electoral roll does exactly what it says on the tin: it's a list of electors – or voters. Every address in a town or city is on it, and next to it are the names of the people that live there. That's so they know who's old enough to vote and stuff, and how many people live in the house. There's a copy in the public library.'

'There, Nia. Your question answered! Say "thank you, SG".'

'Thank you, SG,' I obediently parroted.

'Right, you lot, save your work and pack up ready for lunch.'

I gave Mael a huge grin as I logged off my computer, and he grinned back.

We sat together at lunchtime, tucked away in the corner with our ham baguettes, which were a bit like dry face-flannel lined with pink plastic, if you can imagine it.

Mr Williams popped in for a bottle of water and saw us. He came over. 'Mael, three o'clock in my room, all right? And I can spare you a bit of extra time after school.'

'Thanks, sir. I'll be there.'

Mr Williams grinned and walked off.

'Tell you what, Mael,' – I shoved my lunch away – 'I'll go to the library and see what I can find out and then I'll wait for you back at Aunty Gwenny's.'

Then I saw Ryan O'Brien watching me from behind the cold-drinks machine. I looked away. I felt my face get hot, and knew I looked like a ripe tomato. Then I thought, *why should I worry? I've done nothing wrong. I've got nothing to be ashamed about.* So I gave him a good glare instead. He ducked his head and turned to leave the canteen, then changed his mind and came over. I felt Mael tense, and put my hand on his arm to calm him.

Ryan saw the gesture and faltered, then came over anyway. 'You still trying to make out you aren't going out with him?' he said accusingly. 'Yeah, right.'

'IF it's any of your business, Ryan O'Brien, he's my

cousin, and he's living with my aunt, and I'm making sure he knows his way round school.'

'Yeah? Cousins who wander around in the woods together, right?'

Mael pushed his chair back and stood up. 'I don't like people calling Nia a liar,' he said softly. His head was lowered, his eyes were slitted and they were glinting dangerously. At least he hadn't started sprouting fangs or hair yet. I gave the side seam of his trouser leg a hard tug to remind him he was a student and not an incipient (good word, even in a crisis!) werewolf.

'Yes, we went for a walk together. She's my cousin. I don't know how Nia feels about you and I don't care much, but me, I don't like you. So get lost, now, or –'

'Or?' Ryan pulled himself up to his full rugby-playing height. 'Or what?'

'Oh, cut it out, will you, right now!' I squeaked, getting, like, totally panicky. 'Mael, sit down. Ryan, whatever you think, I don't care. Just go away, will you?'

But of course I did care, and when he turned on his heel I felt horrible. I wanted to run after him and say, 'I really like you, so please will you forgive me?' But forgive me for what? I hadn't done anything, had I? So I bit my lip, collected my school bag and stalked out of the canteen.

After school I headed for the library. The librarians all know me; I'm there every week changing my library books. The nice reddy-blonde one, Carolyn, was on duty. 'Hello, Nia – have you brought any books back? Should I go and take my coffee break now?' That's what she always says because I usually have a great pile of books.

'Not this time. I want to have a look at the electoral roll, if I can, please. Is it allowed, or do I have to be older and have permission and stuff?'

'I don't think so. Anyone can look at it – you don't have to be voting age or anything. I'll get it for you.'

She came back with a huge loose-leaf binder. 'It's up-to-date – I checked, and the amendments have been done quite recently.'

'Why are there amendments?'

'Well, people move away, or die even, and other people move in and then they have to go on the roll instead.'

'Oh. I see.'

I took the book over to one of the big tables and sat down with it. I paged through until I found Cwmparc Street, ran my finger down the column on the left until I got to number 23 – and there it was.

LEIGHTON, Ivor Herbert	Fitter & Turner	
	(Unemployed)	46
LEIGHTON, Maureen Pamela	Housewife	42
LEIGHTON, Beauregard DeCourcy		19
LEIGHTON, Tallulah Marie		17

Beauregard DeCourcy? I couldn't help sniggering at that. I made a quick note of the name – and the spelling – on the cover of my English workbook, so I wouldn't forget it (I mean, was I likely to? I don't *think* so! but I wrote it just the same). There was no occupation listed for him or his sister, so they were both jobless – unless you count mugging old ladies as employment. I gave the book back to Carolyn, and, still smirking, headed for Aunty Gwen's house.

CHAPTER TWENTY-FOUR

B Y THE time I got back, Steffan was already sitting in front of the telly with a glass of pop in one fist and a massive piece of chocolate cake in the other.

'Aunty Gwen, have you been baking?' I asked accusingly.

She looked guilty. 'Yes – with Steffan coming over for tea I had to have a bit of cake to give him, didn't I? I've always got some cake for Steffan, haven't I, lovely?'

Steffan mumbled something appreciative through cake crumbs.

I rolled my eyes. 'You're supposed to be convalescing, Aunty Gwen.'

She looked mutinous. 'I'm all right. Don't fuss, Nia. Nothing wrong with me. Anyway, what's it take to make an old bit of a cake?' Steffan was engrossed in a cartoon, and behind his back she mouthed, '*Where's Mael?*' at me.

'*Extra English,*' I mouthed back. '*He'll come in the back way.*'

'Who will?' Steffan enquired, without removing his eyes from the screen. 'Who's getting extra English?'

Hey, maybe the kid DOES have superpowers!

Then he grinned up at me. 'Oh, I get it. You're talking about him, yeah? That Ryan bloke. Nia's got a boyfriend, Nia's got a boyfriend, Nia's got a boyf—'

'Oh, shut up. If it's any of your business, he isn't my boyfriend any more.' *If he ever was. One rugby match, and a visit to the cinema?* But he was a potential boyfriend, and I didn't even have that now. I felt a bit sniff-er-ly, and might have gone upstairs and had a bit of a bawl if I hadn't heard the faint squeak of the back door's hinges. I winced and Aunty Gwen twitched. We exchanged glances, but luckily Steffan didn't seem to have heard.

Dad collected him at around six o'clock, and when he'd gone, Mael came out of the cellar. He bounded up the steps as soon as Gwenny called him, and gave her a big hug. 'What's to eat?' he enquired. 'I'm starving.'

I did a quick inventory of the freezer in the cellar, found a frozen lasagne, zapped it in the microwave to defrost it, then chucked it in the oven to cook while I washed salad to go with it. 'And there's chocolate cake, if Steffan hasn't eaten it all.'

He hadn't, and if there's one thing that Aunty Gwen makes really well, it's chocolate cake. It's all moist and gorgeous and chocolaty and – almost certainly – horrendously fattening. I can feel the zits popping out on my face just looking at it. We sat at the kitchen table afterwards and burped until our dinner had gone down.

'Did you go to the library?' Mael asked.

'I did.'

'And?'

'Like, total success. Were you expecting anything less?'

'Bighead. So?'

'What are you talking about, you two?' Aunty Gwen asked.

'Well, last night, after you were asleep, Mael and I tracked down where one of the muggers lives.'

'What? You went out in the middle of the night? Nia, anything could have happened to you, wandering around on your own!'

'Not with a werewolf for a bodyguard,' Mael reminded her.

'Oh. Yes. You're right. Silly me! Well – what did you find out? How did you know where to look?'

'Well, you know Mrs Cadwallader's shop was burgled, too, and she was hit over the head and ended up in hospital, like you?'

'No! Nobody told me that! Oh, poor Mrs Cadwallader! Is she all right?'

'I think she'll be OK, but she was really shaken up. Anyway, one of the yobs that did it left his baseball cap behind, caught on a bush outside the shop. Mael smelled it and knew it belonged to the boys that broke in here –'

Oops. I hoped she'd forgotten that bit . . .

'*They broke in here?*'

'Well, not exactly broke in, Aunty – they had your keys, remember?'

'Anyway, Nia,' Mael interrupted, 'what about the address? Did you find out his name?'

'Oh, I did, I did. His name, believe it or not, is Beauregard DeCourcy Leighton.'

'Is it indeed?' Aunty Gwen said. 'I know that lot, the Leightons. That family's notorious – bunch of ne'er-do-wells, they are. Waste of space, the lot of them if you ask me!'

'So, what now?' I asked. 'We've got his name and address and his hat, and we know without any doubt that it was him – but how can we prove it to the police? We still can't just go and hand it in, can we? They'll want to know how we know who it belongs to, won't they?'

'Aunty Gwen, would you know the boys again if you saw them?' Mael asked.

'Oh, indeed I would. Etched on my poor brain forever those two faces are. Now you mention it, that one boy did have the look of the Leightons about him! Eyes much too close together, eyebrows that meet in the middle. And gingery, and squinted a bit. You can never trust a person whose eyebrows meet in the middle, that's what I always say.'

'If we can get the police to be suspicious of one of them, somehow, give them some evidence, maybe they'll arrest him and he'll rat on the other one. What did he call him, Mael?'

Mael thought. 'Dwayne,' he said.

'That's probably Arnold Beech's lad,' Aunty Gwen said. 'He's got a lad called Dwayne, and there aren't many of those around. I was in school with Arnie Beech, and he was a Bad Lot if ever there was one. Like father like son.'

'So, how can we land him in it with the cops?' I persisted.

Aunty Gwen thought for a minute, then her face broke into a marvellous smile. 'Have you still got the hat?' she asked.

'Yes. Of course.'

'Then you fetch it, Mael, and you, Nia, find my sewing box.'

Like, totally mystified, we did as we were told. Aunty Gwen rummaged about in the concertina box on legs that was crammed full with bits of knicker elastic, old buttons, reels of cotton and crochet hooks, and came up with a length of white tape. Right at the bottom she found an ancient sort of pen, and a spool of black thread and a needle. Very carefully, she wrote 'B. DeC. Leighton' in tiny handwriting, then stitched it into the hat. She bent creakily to the hearth and got some ash from the grate and rubbed some of it into the label. When she'd finished, it looked as if it had been there for ever. 'There,' she said, satisfied. 'The police can hardly argue if they've got a hat with his name in it, can they?'

'You sneaky old – lady,' I said admiringly. 'I'd never have thought of that in a million years!'

'Well no, you wouldn't, would you? But then, you never sewed nametapes into every item of clothing your mammy had when she was little, did you?'

She was right: I hadn't.

'But how are we going to get this to the police?' Mael asked.

'Easy. I'll take it in,' I said.

'But how are you supposed to have got hold of it?'

'I found Mrs Cadwallader after she was burgled. I called the ambulance. I'll just tell them the truth – I found it outside the shop and wondered if it might just belong to one of the robbers. Simple!'

'But very effective,' Mael said, half grinning – um – wolfishly.

'I'll drop in at the police station after school tomorrow.

Let's just hope they have enough brains to look inside the cap and find the name.'

And I would have done, I would have. But, as someone once said, 'Life is what happens to you while you're busy making other plans.'

*

Next morning Mael was ridiculously excited: he had his first games lesson, and couldn't wait to start playing rugby. And I was excited too, on his behalf, because he was so chuffed about it . . . *I wasn't thinking straight, was I?*

He had games after lunch, and I had art. I was on my knees, scrambling around my collage, happily gluing myself to the floor and getting paint in my eyebrows, when history repeated itself. The school secretary came looking for me. Not because of a phone call this time, but an 'accident' on the rugby field.

Accident? Yeah, right.

'You'd better come, Nia,' she fussed. 'Your cousin is asking for you. Is it all right, Mrs Richards, if Nia goes to the hospital with him? I tried ringing your parents, Nia, but I couldn't get hold of them. I tried your aunt, but she isn't answering her phone. I left a message on the answerphone for your mum and dad, but . . .'

Oh, double trouble! I thought. My parents were going to be really mystified by a message on their answerphone about a non-existent nephew, weren't they? And Aunty Gwen would be worried stiff if she played back the message on hers. A plague on all efficient secretaries – especially Mrs Wells!

'I'll come right now.' I scrambled to my feet. Mrs Richards handed me a damp cloth and I wiped my hands with it. 'Where's Mael?'

'On the sports field. I've phoned for an ambulance. It should be here any minute now.'

I sprinted outside, across the drive and onto the field. There was a huddle of staff in the middle, and a shape lying on the ground. I skidded to a halt, and looked down at Mael, dead white, his eyes closed.

'What happened?'

'Clash in the line out,' said Torturer Tim. 'I think his leg might be broken, and he certainly got a bit of a bang on the head.'

I glanced around at the gaggle of muddy, scruffy boys in rugby strip standing around awkwardly at the side of the field. Mouthy Morris. Dubious Mike. And Ryan. All trying – and failing – to look innocent. There had been dirty work. They knew it, I knew it, and they knew I knew it.

Mael, hearing my voice, opened his eyes. 'Nia?'

'It's OK, Mael. You'll be fine.'

'Will you come in the ambulance with me?'

Mr Timothy scowled, but I ignored him and said, 'Yeah, of course I will.' I was going, and no one was going to stop me.

The ambulance arrived, and Mael was stretchered into the back of it. I climbed in with him, the doors were slammed, the siren started and off we went to hospital. The paramedic was a girl in her early twenties, and she gave Mael a tube mouthpiece to suck on, to give him a bit of pain relief.

When her back was turned, Mael pulled the mouthpiece out and whispered, 'Don't let them take any blood! And don't let them give me a general anaesthetic!'

'Why?' How was I going to prevent something like that? As far as I knew, they had to get a consent form signed by a parent or guardian before they could do anything operation-ish, but Aunty Gwen wasn't a legal parent or guardian, only a self-appointed one. I was going to have to wing this. 'I won't. But why?' I mouthed back.

'Think about it, Nia!' he hissed, one eye on the paramedic. 'Funny blood? And if I'm unconscious, I'm not going to be in control, am I?'

Oh, shoot! *Now* I got it. If Mael were under a general anaesthetic, he might not be able to stop himself changing. We'd have to talk them into a local anaesthetic to set the leg, or – or they'd have to move him to the nearest vet . . .

CHAPTER TWENTY-FIVE

At THE hospital, Mael, silent and white-lipped, was wheeled into Accident and Emergency. Nice Dr Shami was on duty again, and she looked a bit surprised when she saw me. 'Mrs Furnival's niece, isn't it?' she asked, smiling. 'Have you brought me another customer?'

'Yup!' I said, grinning back. 'Don't want you to get bored.'

'Not much chance of that,' she sighed, glancing round the waiting area, which was as busy as a miserable anthill. 'This young man is obviously in pain. Put him in cubicle,' – she glanced up at a whiteboard – 'five, please.'

The ambulance paramedics slid him behind some curtains and they and Dr Shami gently shifted him between them onto a wheelie-trolley. Mael groaned as they slid him from bed to bed.

I took his hand. He squeezed it tightly.

'Cool head now,' I muttered.

'I'm trying,' he muttered back.

'Would you prefer to wait outside?' Dr Shami suggested.

'Can I stay, please?' I begged. 'Mael's my cousin, and – um – his parents are living abroad.'

'All right. But if you feel faint, sit down.'

As if. I'm not the fainting type, not in hospitals, anyway.

Dr Shami looked at Mael's head first, where a vast purple egg was rising like the sun. 'You had a nasty bump; that must be X-rayed, I think.' Then she turned to his lower half. 'And the leg is almost certainly broken. Right, X-ray for this patient, please, nurse. Meantime, I'll give you something stronger for the pain.'

'No . . . I'm fine,' Mael groaned.

'Are you certain?'

'Yes.'

So off we whizzed to X-ray, me galloping alongside the trolley, still clutching Mael's hand. In the X-ray department several people sat glumly around, hanging on to various bits of themselves as if they were constructed of spun glass. I prepared myself for a long wait but because Mael had an injury to the head, he got whisked in first. I wasn't allowed in with him, so I waited outside and hoped that nothing wolfish would show up on the scan! But when he was wheeled out again, the nurse was still smiling, so his bones must have looked normal. We hung around a bit until the big brown envelope with the films emerged, then we whizzed back to Casualty again.

Dr Shami stuck the pictures on the light-frame and peered at them. 'No skull fractures, luckily – but the leg – that is a very bad break. We shall take you down to theatre and set it under a general anaesthetic . . .'

'No!' Mael and I yelped simultaneously.

'But it would be best –'

'No, really it wouldn't,' I insisted. 'Mael is – is – um – he's horribly allergic to general anaesthetics. He once had a general anaesthetic and reacted very badly.'

'Oh?' Dr Shami said, intrigued. 'What was the anaesthetic for?'

I looked helplessly at Mael.

'Appendicitis,' he supplied.

Dr Shami lifted his jersey and peered at his belly. There was a faint scar there. 'Ah yes. So I see. Who is your GP?'

'He hasn't got one yet,' I ad-libbed. 'He's only just come from abroad to live with my aunt and she hasn't been around to register him.'

'Well, in the absence of any medical records, I think I must take your word for it. I will set your leg under local anaesthetic. But as well as painkillers you must have something to calm you before I begin.'

'What, like a tranquilliser?' I asked, worried again.

'Yes.'

'No . . . I don't need it,' Mael groaned. 'I'm really, really relaxed, honest. Look how calm I am!'

Dr Shami shrugged. 'Well, it might be a bit painful . . . but that leg must be treated without delay.'

I sat holding Mael's hand – he was in a lot of pain despite the local anaesthetic – while Dr Shami and another doctor pulled and tugged his leg around, got it back into roughly the right shape, and whacked a plaster on it, foot to thigh. Eventually, it looked like they'd finished.

'Can he go home now?' I asked.

'No, I am afraid not.' Dr Shami shook her head. 'Because he has had a bump to his head I shall need to keep him in overnight to make sure there is no concussion.'

Oh, rats. 'But I can't stay here overnight!' I wailed. 'I have to get back to my aunty – she's only just out of hospital!'

'I know that. But Mael is a big boy – I expect he'll survive a night in hospital without you, won't you, Mael?'

He might, I thought, *but will you?* I tried to remember if there was a full moon and whether he'd mentioned that he could stop himself changing during them, but drew a blank on both counts. What if he 'werewolfed' in his sleep? Oh, I could almost see the headlines . . .

'Go on. I'll be fine,' Mael urged.

'There you are!' Dr Shami smiled. 'You can come back and visit him tonight.'

At last they found Mael a bed on a ward, and once he was settled with a cradle over his leg and some pills for his aches and pains, I left him and went home to Aunty Gwen.

Who wasn't in.

She was supposed to be convalescing! Where on earth could she have gone? Maybe she'd gone round to our house for some reason. But there'd be nobody in. After all, Mrs Wells had phoned my parents and had had to leave a message! Aaargh! She'd left a message on the answerphone, hadn't she, *saying that their nephew Mael had had an accident and been taken to hospital?* I had to get home and erase it before Mam or Dad played it back.

I probably broke all speed records on the way home. I had a stitch, was cross-eyed and gasping by the time I got to the back door and let myself in. No sign of Aunty Gwen. I bolted into the kitchen and played back the message Mrs Wells had left, then erased it. Saved! I could sit down, have a cup of tea and try to think where on earth Aunty might be.

Then I realised that Steffan would be pitching up on her doorstep any minute now and the house was all shut up and nobody home. He'd have to sit in the garden until I got back. Ah well, at least it wasn't raining. I didn't bother with the tea. I just put my head in my hands and racked my brains. Where on earth could Gwenny be?

Then the phone rang: I threw myself at it, hoping it was Aunty Gwen ringing to tell me she was home. It wasn't. Unreality went into overdrive as a gruff male voice asked to speak to one of my parents.

'Sorry, Mam and Dad aren't here. Who's calling?'

'Sebastopol Road Police Station, miss. We've got a lady here. I think she's your aunt.'

'You WHAT? Is she all right?'

'Perfectly all right, miss. No need to worry. But we need someone to come and collect her.'

'She hasn't had an accident or collapsed or anything? She's only just come out of hospital.'

'So I understand, miss. No, she's perfectly all right – but someone has to take responsibility for her before we let her go. Can you get your mam or dad to come in and get her, please?'

'I don't know when they'll be back. I'll come.'

'Very well. Tell the desk sergeant who you are.'

I hung up and rested my aching head against the cool wall-tiles. What next? Ambulance, hospital, now the police station. I only needed the fire brigade and I'd have a complete set of emergency services, all in one day!

I sprinted round to Sebastopol Road and skidded through the front door. The desk sergeant didn't budge from his paperwork until he'd finished his paragraph, then put his finger on his place and looked up. I didn't interrupt him. Rule number one: never upset a police officer.

'Help you, miss?'

'Yes, my aunt's here – Mrs Furnival?'

'Oh, yes. So she is. Come with me, love – she's just having a cup of tea in her cell.'

'In her *cell? You locked my aunty in a cell?*'

'Ho yes. Even pensioners can't behave like that and get away with it!'

'*Like what?*'

He opened a door and stood back for me to go through. 'Causing a disturbance.'

'*What did she do?*' I was imagining all sorts of terrible things.

'I'll let her tell you that.' And he'd say no more.

Aunty Gwen was sitting sipping a cup of tea. A plate of Jaffa cakes was on a little table beside her (and I doubt tea and Jaffa cakes are usual police-cell issue!). She looked up as the door opened and smiled. 'Oh, Nia dear! I was just telling the nice policewoman all about you.'

The police officer grinned. 'She was indeed.'

I couldn't be bothered to say the usual *all good stuff, I hope.* 'Aunty Gwen, *what did you do?*'

My elderly aunt put down her cup, patted her perm and raised her eyebrows. 'I stood up for myself, Nia dear, that's what. I wasn't having some lout thinking he could knock me about and get away with it! So I Did Something. No offence, dear,' – she patted the police officer's knee – 'I know how busy you are, but if I'd waited for you, I'd . . .'

My stomach churgled. '*What did you do?*' I whispered.

Aunty Gwen smiled smugly. 'I went round to his house. I showed him, and his nasty family. I did indeed. He won't bother me again, I can tell you!'

'Your aunt took the law into her own hands. She had an idea that this boy –'

'Beauregard DeCourcy Leighton,' Aunty Gwen supplied helpfully.

'Yes, him. She imagined he was the one who attacked her and stole her pension the other day –'

'Imagined? I'm not stupid, young woman. It was him, I know it. So I went and had a word with him.'

The policewoman hid a grin. 'Well, you did a bit more than that, Mrs Furnival. You nearly battered the door down, and then you confronted both Beauregard and his father. You were really quite abusive. Threatening even. The arresting officer said he hadn't heard language like that since he was in the army!'

'Quite right too!'

Oh no! I sank down on the hard bed in the cell, fighting an urge to curl up in a ball and suck my thumb. 'What happens now?'

'Well, we'll let her out, now that you've come to fetch her. Luckily, they're not going to press charges.'

'I should think not!' Aunty Gwen said indignantly.

'You were very lucky, actually. You could have found yourself up on a charge of criminal damage.' The police officer stood up. 'Can we have a word outside, miss?'

Numbly I followed her through the door.

'I think your aunt needs to be watched a bit more closely,' she whispered. 'She seems a bit – well – eccentric. Do you think she understands that she can't go round confronting people on a vague suspicion?'

'But it isn't a vague suspicion!' I blurted.

She narrowed her eyes. 'What do you mean?'

Swiftly I explained all about how I'd found Mrs Cadwallader, about the baseball cap snagged on the twigs outside the shop, and the nametape inside the cap (I crossed my fingers for that bit!).

'Do you still have the hat?'

'Of course! It's at Aunty Gwen's house.'

The police officer gazed at me: her face was fairly unreadable. 'A nametape, you say?'

I nodded, trying to look innocent.

'A nametape, in Beauregard DeCourcy Leighton's baseball cap; is that what you're saying?'

'Hmm-hm.' I couldn't say yes; it just wouldn't come out, and I knew I was going pink with the effort of not lying.

'A hand-stitched, neatly lettered nametape. With his name on? Beauregard Leighton?' I won't say she looked suspicious, but when I thought about it, it did sound a bit unlikely. 'Hmmm. Is that so? Well, we'll see. Right now I'll find someone to take you and your aunt home. We'll talk about the hat tomorrow and you can make a statement – if you're really sure you want to. Mind, since your aunt has identified him as one of the people who attacked her, we'll have to interview him anyway . . . Maybe he'll confess and the hat evidence, which you have to admit is just a bit unlikely, may not be necessary.'

Maybe I wouldn't have to perjure myself – and maybe this horrendous day might turn out all right after all!

Then again – it wasn't over yet . . .

CHAPTER TWENTY-SIX

I'D ALWAYS wanted a ride in a police car, and at last I got one! I tried to get the driver to put the siren and flashy lights on, but he wouldn't. Some people have no sense of adventure. He helped Aunty Gwen out of the back seat outside her front door and turned to me. 'Do you want to give me this hat then, love?' he suggested.

I whizzed inside and got it, though it didn't seem like such a good idea any more. I wished Aunty Gwen had never thought of it.

He took it, glanced at the nametape inside the hat and then shot a sideways look at Aunt Gwenny. 'Beautiful,' he said, with the ghost of a smile.

Aunty Gwen met his eyes. Her face was perfectly open, calm and tranquil. 'Who'd have thought a family like that would bother with nametapes?'

'Who indeed?' he said solemnly, and drove away.

Steffan, who was waiting by the back door, was severely cheesed off that I'd ridden in a police car and he hadn't, and whinged about it until I shut him up by feeding him. When we'd all eaten, I settled Gwenny in her armchair with a cup of tea (I'd tell her about Mael later, when Steffan was in bed). Then I got out my homework and spread my books out on the kitchen table. I was about to get down to it when the phone rang in the hall. 'I'll get it, Aunty Gwen,' I carolled. 'Hel-looo? Mrs Furnival's residence.'

'Oh, for goodness' sake, Nia, it's me!'

'Ceri?'

'Nia, it's a disaster! It's happened!'

'What has?' For a minute I couldn't think what she was on about – my head was still full of Aunty Gwen and a werewolf lying in a ward in an NHS hospital.

'Mam. She's found out!'

Then I remembered. 'Oh, no! How?'

'We were doing the hospital scene.' (I went blank for a sec. at that point, my head being full of hospitals anyway.) 'She was on a trolley, being a victim, all covered in blood and gore, and I was supposed to be interviewing her to get details about her attacker. I managed to persuade the director to let me wear a surgical mask – yes, I know it sounds unlikely – but it wasn't any good; as soon as I spoke she recognised my voice.'

'Oh, no! What did she do?'

'Came up off her deathbed like an avenging angel, ripped off my mask and screamed blue murder.'

I slithered down the wall and held my head, the receiver still clamped to my ear. 'And?'

'The director stopped the filming and wanted to know what was going on. Mam was screeching like a banshee, and Pietro, Pete, was standing around with his mouth open, looking from me to her, and – oh, Nia, it was horrible. What am I going to do?'

'More to the point, what's the director going to do?'

'He's already done it,' she said miserably. 'He sacked Mam.'

'And you?'

'No. I'm the female lead, aren't I? I'd be too expensive to replace. Besides, I didn't do anything, did I?'

'What did Mam say?'

'She said I'd ruined her career and blighted her life, and then she ran out of the studio. I haven't seen her since. Can you check she's got home safe and then ring me back?'

'Why? Do you want to avoid her or see her?'

'I don't know. I just want to know she's all right. I suppose I should apologise, but –'

'Why should you, Ceri? You haven't done anything wrong.'

'But I have – and for her to find out like that, and then get sacked as a result . . . Oh, I should have known better than to try to keep it a secret.'

'You've got a right to your own life, Ceri.' I racked my brains to try to think of something encouraging to say. 'Anyway, if Mam was a true professional, she'd have stayed in character and wouldn't have thrown a wobbly and got sacked. Actors have to act even if they're dying. The Show Must Go On and that.'

'Well it didn't; it came to a full stop. Look, Nia, be an angel, ring home and find out if she's there – then I'll decide what to do. I s'pose,' she finished, miserably, 'I ought to go home and explain.'

'OK. I'll ring you back. What number are you on?'

She rattled off a number I didn't recognise. 'What number's that, then?'

'Pete's mobile.'

'What? You've got his mobile?'

'Yeah. My battery's flat. I – oh, never mind that, Nia – just do it, will you?'

I hung up and dialled home. No answer. Dad was off on business; Mam wasn't in. So where was she? I rang Ceri back. 'No one's home.'

There was silence at the other end.

'I'll go home then. Nia, will you come too? I need some moral support if I'm going to face up to Mam and Dad. She's bound to turn up sooner or later. Where else could she go?'

'OK. I'm on my way.' I hung up again and went into the living room, where Aunty Gwen and Steffan were watching telly side by side. 'Look, I've got to go home for a while, Aunty Gwen. I'll be back soon as I can. Will you be all right?'

'Of course. I'm not helpless, am I? Besides, Steffan is here to look after me, aren't you, dear?'

He grinned. 'Yeah. Course I am. I'm staying here tonight, Ni.'

I scowled at him. 'Right. Behave yourself, Steff, and bed no later than nine, all right? And no computer games after you're in bed, you hear?'

He rolled his eyes. 'Yeah, right. Who do you think you are, Nia? Mam?'

Just as well I wasn't. He had no idea what was going on.

Gwenny waited until his head was turned towards the telly, then mouthed, 'Where's Mael?'

'Tell you later!' I mouthed back.

I let myself out of the house and headed home. Sprinting past Mrs Cadwallader's shop, I spotted three familiar figures. I stopped, narrowed my eyes. Mouthy Morris, Dubious Mike and Ryan O'Brien. Mouthy saw me, and smirked. 'How's the boyfriend, then, Nia?'

'Shut up, Mouthy,' Ryan muttered, turning pink.

'Well,' Mouthy said, grinning openly now, 'not every day someone's unlucky enough to break their leg playin' rugby, is it?'

That did it. I marched up to the three of them, drew myself up to my full height (five-feet-nothing) and started. 'I hope you're proud of yourselves. You did it deliberately, I know you did! You make me sick, the lot of you. Mael's in hospital because of you, with a broken leg and concussion. You could have killed him. You can count yourselves lucky he didn't –' I was going to say, 'tear you limb from limb,' but I managed to stop myself just in time – 'um, press charges,' I finished lamely.

'Yeah, right,' Dubious Mike sneered. 'Like he's going to go to the police over a rugby injury. They'd laugh at him, specially round here.'

'Yeah, I can just see it.' Mouthy put on a high-pitched voice: 'You see, officer, I was playing this nasty rough game and I got a little bump. Arrest them, officer. Take them away.'

Ryan hadn't said a word. I turned on him. 'You haven't got much to say for yourself, Ryan, have you? Proud of yourself, is it? You're as much to blame as they are – you were in on it too, so don't make out you weren't. I'm gonna tell you just one last time. Mael's my friend. Nothing more, nothing less. He's not my boyfriend or anything like it. He's my cousin. We're good mates. Got it? And if you can't hack that, then I'm sorry: it's your problem and not mine.'

He nodded, bright red. 'But –'

'But nothing, Ryan O'Brien. I thought you were better than that, but you aren't. I don't care if I never set eyes on you again. You're cowards, all three of you. And bullies. And if there's one thing lower than a coward, it's a bully.'

I turned and left the three of them open-mouthed and, in Ryan's case, crimson-faced. Once I was round the corner I started to run again. The front door was open: somebody was home then. Once I heard the shrieks, I knew they both were. I burst through the kitchen door and found Mam and Ceri eyeball to eyeball and nose to nose. Mam was wearing a red-stained bandage round her head and her face was covered in fake cuts and bruises.

'How have I ruined your career, Mam? You didn't have one!' Ceri was screaming.

'You're only in the film because of that Italian person, aren't you! He fixed it for you, didn't he? What do you know about acting?'

'That's not true, Mam! I got the part before I even met Pete! He had nothing to do with it!'

'I don't believe you, Ceri! I hope you're satisfied. Anyway, what makes you think you can even act?'

'An agent, a producer and a director!' Ceri screamed back. 'That's who! I did a screen test and an audition and they offered me the part! I didn't just turn up as a –'

I just knew she was about to say something like 'lousy, pathetic extra', and I knew if she said it that she and Mam would never be the same again, ever. I couldn't stand by and let her say what we all thought about Mam's acting: that Mam's dream was all pie-in-the-sky, that she'd only ever be an extra and an unconvincing one at that, and she might as well give up now and forget it.

I looked round, wildly. Shouting wouldn't help: they were yelling too loudly to hear me, so I grabbed Mam's Portmeirion fruit bowl, raised it over my head and dashed it onto the kitchen tiles. There was a loud explosion of sound, bits of shattered pottery shot in all directions, and the shouting stopped as if I'd thrown a switch.

'That's better,' I wheezed, still suffering from the sprint down the road. 'Do you want the neighbours to know everything that goes on in this house? Stop it, the pair of you. Screaming like a pair of fishwives. You should be ashamed of yourselves.' I didn't actually know what fishwifely screaming was like, but it sounded good.

Ceri and Mam turned to me with identical sulky expressions.

'You have no idea –' Mam began.

'D'you know what she's –' Ceri said simultaneously.

'SHUT UP!' I interrupted, and to my amazement, they did. 'Just shut up, will you, and listen.' I didn't have a clue what I was going to say, but amazingly, the words came. 'Look, both of you, sit down,' I begged, and after glaring at each other for a bit, they sat, lower lips still stuck out. 'Mam, Ceri didn't tell you about her part in the series because she knew you'd be upset. And she was right: you are. We all know how much you want to act, and Ceri felt guilty –'

Ceri looked up at me then, and opened her mouth, but shut it again when I scowled at her.

'– Ceri felt guilty because she just got a lucky break, that's all. She was spotted in a caff, having a coffee, and you were never lucky enough for that to happen to you. You're both stars – um – in your own way,' (and, oh boy, did I have my fingers tightly crossed behind my back right then!) 'but Ceri got the break, Mam. You didn't. You're her mother,' – time to play the Mam card now. 'Aren't you proud of her? Obviously,' I went on, 'she got her talent from you. You must be, like, really proud of that. Without your genes, Mam, she'd never be an actress.'

Ceri's eyebrows were going up and down like skyrockets on Guy Fawkes, but Mam was Thinking.

'It's not just the acting,' she said eventually. 'She's keeping secrets from her dad and me. I mean, Ceri, going out with someone like that Italian boy –'

'He's not "that Italian boy", Mam. He's –'

'Don't interrupt,' I said, and she shut up.

'Anything could have happened. You're only nineteen, Ceri; you don't know what the world's like yet –'

Ceri rolled her eyes and sighed.

'But as for the acting, Nia's right. Without my example, my genes, my talent, you'd never even have thought about acting, would you? Your talent, your ability, you inherited – no, you *learned* that from me, didn't you?'

Ceri opened and shut her mouth, spluttering.

Don't you dare say a word! I thought at her. *Just agree with her, will you?* Thank goodness she picked it up.

'Yes, Mam,' she said demurely, lowering her eyes – just as well Mam couldn't see her expression (she wasn't that good an actress!) – 'without you, I'd never even have thought of it. You can take all the credit, Mam.'

A smile appeared on Mam's face. Her hair was standing

on end under the bandage and fake blood was trickling down her nose. 'Well, my darling, let this be a lesson to you,' she said, giving Ceri a messy hug, 'not to keep secrets. Truth will out!' she said dramatically. 'And if you need any advice or help with your part . . . you will ask, won't you, darling?'

'She will,' I said, quickly, before Ceri could explode. 'Won't you, Ceri?'

She glared at me. 'Yeah,' she said. She managed a sweet smile. Maybe she *could* act, my sister! I let out a huge, relieved sigh. Navigated that one, then! At last the Big Secret (well, one of them, anyway) was out in the open and I wouldn't have to worry about Dad letting anything slip. Maybe life could get back to normal now.

Then the kitchen phone rang.

CHAPTER TWENTY-SEVEN

I WAS nearest so I got to the phone first. Lucky, because it was Dr Shami. What she said made me go cold all over. Mael had disappeared.

'The ward sister noticed he was very restless,' the doctor said, her voice tired. 'He kept thrashing about and muttering a lot of nonsense, so she sent for me to have a look at him – mainly because of his head injury. But I was detained by an emergency, and by the time I reached the ward, his bed was empty. How on earth he managed to get away with his leg in plaster, I can't imagine.'

Unfortunately, I could. While I was on the phone, I'd glanced out the window. There was a full moon . . .

'I thought perhaps the best thing would be to telephone your parents,' Dr Shami went on, wearily. 'If you will tell them, Nia, then I shall telephone the police. They will find him, I'm sure.'

'No!' I yelped. 'Don't call the police! It's all right – he's – he's already phoned us. He decided he didn't want to stay any more – he hates hospitals. He's fine, really he is – he's in a taxi and on his way here. Honest!'

'Oh! I am so relieved!' the doctor said, and I felt really guilty at deceiving her. 'Will you tell him, please, that he has made me very worried? And all for no reason. I am very cross with him. And tell him also that he must not walk on his broken leg. And, Nia, if he should become sleepy, you must make sure that your parents bring him back to the hospital immediately just in case he has concussion.'

'I understand. It's all right. He'll be fine, I'm sure. We'll take care of him.'

I hung up. Mam and Ceri were staring at me.

'Take care of who?' Ceri asked.

'What's going on?' Mam demanded. 'Who was that? What are you up to now, Nia?'

'Nothing, Mam, honest. Look, I've got to go out for a bit.'

'Not at this time of night, you don't.'

'Yes I do. I'm staying with Aunty Gwen. And Steff's over there, remember?'

'Well, of course I do. You still aren't going round there on your own. I'll drive you.'

'You can't, Mam. Dad's taken the car.'

'Oh yes. So he has. He'll be back soon, though, so you can wait until he gets here. I'll just ring Gwenny and tell her –'

'I'll be fine, Mam. Don't worry, all right? Look, I'll phone you as soon as I get there.'

'It's all right, Mam,' Ceri suddenly said. 'I'll go with her. I can always sleep on Aunty Gwen's settee. Hang on while I get my nightie and toothbrush, Ni.'

This was going from bad to worse, but having Ceri tagging along wouldn't be nearly as bad as having Mam asking awkward questions. Besides, Ceri owed me big time. If I could get her to take care of Aunty Gwen, then I could go and look for Mael. I kept telling myself everything would be fine: he was a big boy/wolf; he could look after himself.

Except . . . his leg was broken, he was in pain, and he was out there somewhere.

At last Ceri and I got away. I looked up at the full moon sailing serenely overhead, not at all concerned with what was going on down here. I was starting to panic: I didn't have a clue where to start looking. I had a quick shufti round the front garden in case he'd found his way there, but no such luck.

Ceri hitched her backpack higher on her shoulder. There was more than a nightie and a toothbrush in there! 'All right, Nia, now tell me what's going on,' she demanded.

'Nothing,' I lied.

'Oh, sure, right. I've known you all your life, Nia, and I know when you're worried. *And* when you're lying. And you're lying now. So. What?'

'I don't think you'd understand, Ceri. Honest, you wouldn't. And I don't think you'd believe me if I told you.'

'Try me.'

I sighed a big sigh. *Well. Here goes nothing*, I thought. 'It's Aunty Gwen, Cer. She's, like, got this lodger . . .'

'Aunty Gwen's got a lodger? When did that happen? Who is it?'

'It's a boy. His name's Mael.'

'A *boy*? Aunty Gwen?'

'Yeah. And he broke his leg this afternoon, playing rugby. He was in hospital, but he's sort of disappeared. That was the hospital on the phone just now.'

'How? How can a boy with a broken leg disappear from a hospital? And anyway, what's some strange boy doing, staying with Aunty Gwen?' She stopped walking and stared at me.

'He just is, all right? And I've got to find him. He might have concussion as well, so he can't just wander around. I've really, really got to find him, Cer!'

'He won't be doing much wandering with a broken leg, will he?'

I could hardly tell her that, given the full moon, he probably had three other perfectly usable legs, and could get around quite happily on them if he had to. 'Well,' I hedged, 'it's not quite as simple as that . . .'

Ceri suddenly put out a hand. 'Hang on a minute there, Nia. I think I know what's going on. Gwenny. Lodger. Boy. This is one of Gwenny's waifs and strays, right? Oh, no, not again!'

My turn to stop and stare. 'You what?'

'Oh, Gwenny's famous for it! She was always picking up weird characters and bringing them home.' She tutted and shook her head. 'Still at it, is she? What's this one like? A bit peculiar, I expect?'

'You could say that.' I was beginning to feel vaguely hysterical, as if my head might fly off into outer space any minute now. I couldn't hack this: I know my family's as nutty as peanut brittle – but . . .

'How peculiar?' She didn't wait for me to answer. 'Oh, ye gods, I remember when I was a little, little kid, she had this bloke living in the spare bedroom – what was his name? Alwyn, Elwyn – no, Aelfryn, that's it. Now he was, like, a total weirdo. Disappeared after a bit. Never saw him again, after. Never went out, as far as I could tell. Nice enough chap, but terrible hang-ups. Just the sort Aunty Gwen can't resist.'

Hang-ups? That had to be the understatement of the century! 'You *knew* about him? Did Mam know? Dad?'

'Oh, sure. Aunty Gwen's got a talent for spotting society's misfits. She's a sort of social worker in her own way: if it wasn't people it would be lost dogs or cats or stray donkeys. They mostly seem to be harmless –'

That's all you know! I thought.

'– and they don't ever seem to stay long. She's so secretive about them; it's a bit of a joke. I can't understand why you didn't know – except she hasn't had one for about ooh, seven or eight years, I suppose, so you'd only have been a little kid when that Aelfryn bloke was there. What's the new one like?'

'He's fine. He's – well, I've enrolled him in school. But he broke his leg in this rugby match and he's done a runner from the hospital.'

'Well, a hopper, anyway. I expect he'll find his way home; they usually do.'

'But anything could happen to him! He's out there all on his own!'

'Oh, he'll be all right. He'll hole up somewhere until dawn, I expect, then come home, bringing his tail behind him.'

I didn't say anything. She didn't have a clue how right she was!

'Sorry. Look, what's the worst thing that could happen? He could catch a cold, right?'

'He's in pain, and he might have concussion. We need to find him. But I don't know where to start looking.'

Ceri thought. 'Well, if it were me, I'd probably go to where I felt safe –'

'Aunty Gwen's!' I said, relief flooding me. 'Look, Ceri, you go and stay with Siân. No point in the two of us being at Gwenny's, is there? I'll make sure she's OK. Like you say, I expect he'll turn up sooner or later.' I really didn't think I wanted Ceri getting in the way.

'All right. Ring me at Siân's if you need me.'

Luckily Steffan was in bed when I got to my aunt's house, although I could hear muffled bleeps coming from the spare room. First thing, I rang Mam to tell her I'd arrived safely, then I shot down into the cellar to see if Mael was there. He wasn't, so I opened the cobwebbed back door and went out into the garden. The moon was huge, high and silver, and I wondered if Mael would be able to retain his human shape against the pull of that, no matter how determined he was, especially in his weakened condition and dosed up with painkillers. Light flooded the garden eerily, casting shadows of trees and fruit bushes, and gleaming on the shed roof. He wasn't in there, and though I stood in the garden and called, there was no answering growl, whine or whimper – or even human voice. I looked in the front garden, too, but he wasn't there either.

Gwen looked accusingly at me when I went back into the parlour.

'How did my boy come to break his leg? You told me he'd be safe, going to school with you, but he wasn't, was he, Nia?'

'Well, no. But if there hadn't been a full moon, Aunty Gwen, he'd have been fine.'

'But there *is* a full moon, and the poor wee lamb is out there all alone, in pain and probably terrified.'

The poor wee lamb had a fairly fearsome set of fangs, but apart from that, I could see her point. 'Look, Aunty Gwen, I'm going to go and look for him. Do you think he might be lying up in the woods somewhere?'

'That's more than possible.' She struggled to her feet. 'Fetch me my jacket, Nia. I'm coming with you.'

That was all I needed, my aged aunty staggering around the woods in the dark, tripping over stuff and breaking both her hips. 'No way, Aunty! You stay here. Someone has to stay with Steffan, right? He's only a little boy. And besides, what if Mael should come back and no one's here to let him in?'

Aunty Gwen sat down again. 'All right, Nia, you go, then. Take my torch; it's on the hook inside the cellar door. And better make sure the back door's left open when you go out, so he can get in if he does come here. He has difficulty with doorknobs when he's, you know, *like that.*'

I got the torch and headed off out again. It was only a short walk to the woods, and I climbed over the Forestry Commission stile and headed into the trees. The moon was still bright but it was very dark in the woods. Despite the torch, I stumbled over roots and got torn by brambles. There were also lots of tiny noises – little rustles and squeaks and scrapes – the sort you don't even notice in daylight but which seem Very Loud at night. A barn owl glided over my head and nearly gave me a heart attack.

I bumbled further into the darkness; the moonlight was more diffused now, paler under the thick canopy of trees. Every so often I called Mael's name, but there was no reply.

If he wasn't in the woods, I didn't have a clue where he might be. What if he was dead? Perhaps he couldn't die. He was a werewolf, after all. Didn't they have to get shot by a silver bullet? Or was that just fiction, like the howling and moaning and writhing when they changed shape, and the stuff about being uncontrollable at full moon?

And then I heard vicious snarling, loud barks and harsh voices . . .

I crept towards the sound of the voices, slipping from tree to tree, trying to keep out of sight. I needn't have worried: the men and dogs were far too occupied with what they'd found to notice me creeping about.

What they'd found, of course, was Mael. He was tucked into a hollow made where the trunks of two trees had fallen across each other, crouched back, hackles up, great fangs bared, growls rumbling from deep in his chest. Three men and four dogs surrounded his lair, the dogs barking and snarling hysterically, making leaps towards him on their short leashes. One of the men carried a spade, and they all had shotguns.

Badger baiters! I thought.

One of the men had lifted his gun and was taking aim at Mael. I heard the metallic 'snick' as he cocked the gun.

'Don't shoot it!' one of the other men shouted, knocking the gun up. 'If we can get it alive, we can face it off against the dogs! It'll be a laugh! I ain't seen a good dogfight in months.'

They thought he was a dog! If they set Mael against the hounds, they'd probably come off worse, broken leg or not. I had to act quickly. I stepped out of my hiding place and got my mobile out of my pocket. 'Stop it right now!' I yelled. I just had time to notice that the battery was down to about a quarter strength . . .

The men turned round, and I said it again. 'I know what you're up to. I've phoned the police and they're on their way.'

'Get her!' one of the men shouted, starting forward, but an older man held him back. 'If she's called the pigs, we'd better scarper,' he said. 'Call the dogs off.'

The younger one put his face close to mine. 'I know what you look like, darlin',' he snarled. 'So just you stay out of my way. You won't be so lucky next time.'

I put the phone to my ear. 'Hello? You still there? You heard that?' I listened, calmly, without taking my eyes off the man's face. 'Good. Recorded, too? Excellent. So, the description of the man that just threatened me is –'

They ran for it. Just as well. I was about to faint from sheer terror.

I went stumbling across the rough ground on legs like ice lollies in August. I put the phone back in my pocket. I really did need to remember to put it on charge or next time I was in a situation like this I'd have real problems. Fortunately they didn't guess that there was no one at the other end. The last people I wanted buzzing around were the police.

I'm, like, so nuts, I thought, weakly. *Totally nuts! I'm as mad as the rest of them. Mad as a box of frogs under a full moon. I could have got myself scragged out here!*

The werewolf had collapsed onto his side, completely motionless, only the rise and fall of his chest showing that he was alive. I bent down and shone the torch in under the crossed tree-trunks. The great grey body was stretched out, one hind leg horribly bent out of shape. 'Where's your plaster, Mael?' And then I realised that as soon as he'd

215

changed, of course, it would have fallen off. The plaster had been moulded round a human leg, not a wolf one.

I touched his head, and he turned to look at me. Tears prickled at the back of my eyes. It was horrible to see him so weak and helpless. 'Can you walk on three legs, Mael?'

But it was more than just a broken leg. I shone the torch onto the ground below his body. Blood was seeping slowly onto the dead leaves on the forest floor. 'Did the dogs get you?'

The great head rose and fell in a nod.

'I can't carry you! You're much too heavy. Oh, what can I do, Mael?' I was panicking now. If he was bleeding, he might die before I could get help for him. The great head lifted again, the golden eyes slitted in pain.

I got out the mobile again. 'Mam? It's Nia. Is Dad back yet? Oh, great. Put him on, will you? Hi, Dad?'

I didn't take my eyes off Mael's limp body while I explained the situation as fast as I could in case my phone died. I told him I'd followed this 'big dog' and it was hurt. I arranged to meet him at the entrance to the woods, at the Forestry Commission gate. I switched off the phone and bent over the great creature. 'Hang on, Mael – my dad's coming and we're going to get you out of here.'

CHAPTER TWENTY-EIGHT

Dad got there in record time. He took one look at Mael and raised his eyebrows. 'If that's a dog, I'm a Dutchman,' he commented. 'That's at the very least a wolf-cross. Some fool's let it stray.' He'd thought to bring a big sleeping bag, and we managed to roll Mael onto it. Then I took the front end, Dad took the back, and between us we half-dragged, half-carried Mael back to the car and got him lying across the back seat. I climbed into the front passenger seat, belted up, craning backwards to see him. He was completely still, his eyes closed. Dad hung around outside the car to make a call on his mobile, then he got into the driving seat.

'Where are we going?' I asked, still in a bit of a panic. I wasn't thinking straight, or I wouldn't have said, 'Look, Dad, we – um – can't take him to the hospital!'

'Hospital?' Dad said, puzzled. 'I know that. We're going to the vet's, of course.'

'Oh – yeah, right.' I mentally kicked my own backside. Of course Dad thought Mael was a wolfhound. But – would the vet ask awkward questions? Would he notice anything weird about Mael? How would Mael react? I couldn't risk it. 'Um, Dad,' I hedged. 'What about the dangerous-dogs law-thingy? Isn't it illegal for a wolf-cross to be out without a muzzle? Won't the vet have to report it to the police? They might put him down, if he's half wolf? Dad, we can't let that happen, we can't!'

'Of course not. Not this vet, anyway,' Dad said, grinning. 'We've used him before.'

He had? When? Why? We've never had pets in our house – Mam's allergic to all fur except possibly mink, for which she'd probably gladly suffer death by sneezing.

On the outskirts of the town, he stopped the car outside a big house with a wide drive and a stable block. A curious head poked out of one of the stable doors as we lifted Mael out. The horse whinnied in alarm and ducked back inside as it caught the smell of wolf. The door of the main building opened and a man in a white coat came out, wheeling a short trolley. Between them, he and Dad got Mael onto the trolley and whizzed him into the surgery.

'Good of you to see us,' Dad said, shaking hands with the vet, 'especially at this time of night.'

'No probs,' the vet replied, gently palpating (posh word for 'feeling') Mael's stomach, peering into his eyes and lifting his lips to inspect his gums. 'Haven't seen one of these chaps for a good long time. One of Gwen's, is it?'

'Aye,' Dad replied.

'What?' I asked, bewildered. 'You've seen one before? A wolf, I mean,' I added hastily.

The vet looked up and grinned. 'Oh, come now. We all know he isn't exactly a wolf, don't we?'

'You what?' I said, startled.

'Gwenny doesn't just take in ordinary waifs and strays, Nia,' Dad said. 'She's a bit of an oddball, your aunty. You

218

know exactly what he is, right? He wasn't some stray dog you followed into the woods, now, was he? Come on. Be honest.'

I stared at him. 'You know, Dad? How long have you known?'

'Ever since I've known your mam, lovely girl. Mind you, no one else knows outside the family. But your mam would have a conniption fit if she thought Gwenny was still holding open house for werewolves and vampires, so this stays between us. What's his name?'

'Mael,' I said, still boggling a bit. I decided to ask questions later. 'Is he going to be all right?' I begged. I felt to blame, somehow, for all Mael's problems. If I hadn't had a thing with Ryan O'Brien (the rat!) none of this would have happened.

The vet looked up and smiled. 'I think so. He'll be sore for a bit, and it will hurt like hell when he changes, but it takes a lot to damage one of these chappies seriously.'

The 'chappie' in question raised his head. Tawny almond-shaped eyes gazed into mine. One eye closed in a wink . . .

I felt better after that. We were sent to sit in the waiting room while the vet worked on Mael, and Dad rang Mam so she wouldn't worry when he didn't come straight home. It was dawn, and I was dozing, my head on Dad's shoulder and his arm around me, when the vet opened the clinic door and called us in. Mael, now back in boy shape, was lying, drowsily propped against pillows on the operating table, his leg in plaster and his side stitched and bandaged.

'Good as new,' the vet said. 'I gave him a general anaesthetic when the sun came up, so it wouldn't hurt too much, changing back. He's still a bit groggy, but he'll be fine by tonight. I'll keep him here in the meantime, and you can come and collect him later. Around five, five-thirty? I have a clinic starting at six.'

Mael was gazing at me sleepily. 'Thanks, Nia,' he mumbled, and went to sleep again.

In the car, driving home, I asked Dad all the questions that had been bubbling around in my head. Like, why us? I knew the whole family was potty, but how, who, why, what, where and when did Aunty Gwenny get involved in supernatural beings? And was it just werewolves and vampires?

'Well, love,' Dad explained. 'Aunty Gwen's been a bit sort of "special" since she was a kid, though she put it aside while your mam was small, because children are very aware of stuff like that and it isn't good for them. I've always known about her little hobby, mind. I suppose she's a bit like a magnet for people in trouble. Some people just get society's normal run-of-the-mill misfits. Aunty Gwenny gets the others. She's a sort of –'

'A supernatural social worker?' I asked, grinning.

'Yeah. That'd be it. Only better.'

'But why didn't she want anyone – even you – to know about Mael? Since you obviously knew about it – even if I didn't,' I reminded him indignantly, 'why wouldn't she tell you, at least?'

'Because we banned her from taking in any more,' Dad said.

'Why?'

'Well, one time she got herself infested by a poltergeist, and she brought it round to our house. Not on purpose, you understand, but it came with her – oh, you would only have been a toddler – and it seemed to like our house better than hers. Caused a lot of upset and damage before we managed to get rid of it. For a bit, neither your mam nor me cottoned on to what was happening, so every time something got broken one of you kids got the blame! And I thought, at her age, the whole caboodle was a bit of a risk – to all of us. So I said, "Look, Gwenny, enough's enough."'

Now he mentioned it, I vaguely remembered teddies flying about my bedroom and my doll's house rearranging itself while I watched. 'And Aunty Gwen agreed?'

'I thought she had,' he said grimly. 'I'd absolutely forbidden her to ever do it again, but when she promised she probably had her fingers crossed or something. I imagine she didn't tell me about Mael because she knew I'd get cross with her and put a stop to it. And I would have, still, except Mael is rather younger than the usual sort she takes on. He couldn't possibly fend for himself yet.'

'The question is,' I said, 'what are we going to do about him, now we all know?'

'I don't honestly think he should go on living at Gwenny's,' Dad said. 'She can hardly look after herself, let alone take on a teenage boy. Especially one with problems.'

'But they aren't really problems –'

'Yes they are, Nia,' Dad put in. 'Nine-tenths of the time he's a boy. He needs to be allowed to live like one. With the best will in the world, Gwenny can't really cope, and I don't think she can go on living in that big old house all by herself much longer, either, so what will happen to him then?'

'So what are you suggesting?' I asked indignantly. 'We

put Aunty Gwen into an old folks' home and send Mael to the RSPCA or something?'

Dad sighed. 'Nia, get off your high horse before you come to the jumps, *cariad*. Of course we won't put either of them into a home. Your mam and I were talking about the Gwenny problem before I even knew about Mael.'

'You were?'

'Well, yes. Gwenny's more of a mother to your mam than her real mam ever was. We wouldn't dream of putting her into a home – not while we're able to take care of her. It may be different when she gets very, very old, because of the danger that she might fall or something: we can't watch her every second of the day and night. But until then, she'll come to us.'

'Have we got room?' I asked, doubtfully. 'I'm not being funny, Dad. I'd love to have Gwenny living with us – but where? Us kids have got a room each, and there isn't a spare.'

'We've thought of that. If Gwenny sells her house, we could use the money from that to build her a granny-flat extension in the garden. She could live there and be almost as independent as she is now.'

'But what about Mael?'

'If we're building an extension, love, we might as well make it big enough for two.'

So, that was sorted, then! Dad dropped me off at Gwenny's where I brought her up to date on Mael's progress – nothing else, mind. Dad and Mam could do the ticklish stuff, later. Anyway, Dad had to break it to Mam that she was about to gain a foster son. A son with some weird personal habits, although he probably wouldn't mention that right now!

Everything was OK between Ceri and Mam, although Ceri had to grit her teeth quite often when Mam started talking about the 'acting gene' she'd donated. Ceri managed to wangle it so that Mam got back on set – Pietro thought the whole thing was hilarious once he knew the truth, and he had a word with the director and got her rehired. The director, naturally, didn't want to upset his star, so when the TV series was aired, there was Mam, e-moaning (that's a cross between emoting and moaning) like mad, on her stretcher, with Ceri standing by to catch juicy details about the attacker for the psychological profile.

I thought, well, good for Pietro Annigoni Jones. But I still didn't trust him. Then one night I stuck my head into Ceri's bedroom and found her in floods on the bed. I put my arms round her and patted her. 'That rotten Pietro's dumped you, hasn't he? Oooh, if I could get my hands on him! You were nothing to him, were you?' I said indignantly.

She sat up, fumbled for a tissue and blew her nose. 'Where did you get an idea like that? Nothing's wrong,' she said, wiping her eyes. 'He's asked me to marry him, and I'm just so hap- hap- haaaappyyyy!' And off she went again, sobbing and snorting and snotting.

They got engaged just after the series started, and there was loads about it in the papers. Ceri's going to be in the next series, too. It'll be a while before they get married, but she wants me to be bridesmaid (OK, I get to choose the frock), and Steffan's *possibly* going to be pageboy, although that might take some negotiating ('Like, no way, Ceri!'), and Mael, providing there isn't a full moon, will be an usher . . .

Aunty Gwen and Mael are living with us now, in their nice modern extension, and Aunty Gwen hasn't been in any more trouble. Beauregard DeCourcy Leighton, when interviewed by the police, was swift to mention the name of his co-mugger, and they both went down for aggravated assault or something. Because both Aunty Gwen and Mrs Cadwallader were able to identify their attackers, the police didn't need the nametaped hat as evidence – which was probably just as well.

So, everybody's living happily ever after, then.

Except me. Sigh. Poor me.

Ryan O'Brien keeps popping up wherever I happen to be, with this sheepish little smile on his face. He isn't hanging around with Dubious Mike and Mouthy Morris so much any more, which is good. I think he's trying to pluck up courage to ask me out again.

The question is, am I going to forgive him? What he did was, like, *so totally unforgivable*. And he didn't trust me, did he? He could have got Mael killed, if you think about it. I should probably never forgive him, ever.

But . . .

He is quite cute, even if he does have an obsessive compulsive rugby disorder.

So . . . Since life itself is mad as a box of frogs, maybe I shall. When I think he's suffered enough, that is.

Like – by the next full moon?